LIFE'S A BEACH
OR
A NIGHTMARE

BY

J. N. STEPHENSON

Copyright © J. N. Stephenson 2017
This book is sold subject to the condition that it shall not, by way of trade or otherwise, be lent, resold, hired out, or otherwise circulated without the publisher's prior consent in any form of binding or cover other than that in which it is published and without a similar condition including this condition being imposed on the subsequent publisher.
The moral right of J. N. Stephenson has been asserted.
ISBN-13: 978-1979201834
ISBN-10:1979201838

DEDICATION

This book was inspired by all the people who contacted me wanting more from Jonny's life, so I would like to include them in my dedication as well as my wife Karen and four sons: Dylan, Brad, Ky and Makenzie.

Thank you so much for your patience.

ACKNOWLEDGEMENTS

A special thanks to Harry Ritchie who pulled me out of so many holes.

CONTENTS

CHAPTER 1 *Early Mornings* 1
CHAPTER 2 *Fixtures And Fittings* 8
CHAPTER 3 *Buffaloes* 16
CHAPTER 4 *Opening Night* 26
CHAPTER 5 *A Big Surprise* 35
CHAPTER 6 *The Big Question* 48
CHAPTER 7 *A Quick Change* 55
CHAPTER 8 *I Do* 73
CHAPTER 9 *A Fortnight Early* 85
CHAPTER 10 *40 Winks* 96
CHAPTER 11 *The Phone Call* 102
CHAPTER 12 *The Photo* 109
CHAPTER 13 *The Taste Of Blood* 119
CHAPTER 14 *An Unexpected Visitor* 124
CHAPTER 15 *No Way Out* 133
CHAPTER 16 *Bide My Time* 141
CHAPTER 17 *Regular As Clockwork* 153
CHAPTER 18 *Out Of Order* 167
CHAPTER 19 *The Cover Of Darkness* 177
CHAPTER 20 *Homeward Bound* 187
CHAPTER 21 *Sleeper* 196
CHAPTER 22 *Hardman Harry* 204
CHAPTER 23 *Smiles And Laughter* 215
CHAPTER 24 *High Speed* 224
CHAPTER 25 *Home For Good* 235

This is a work of fiction. Names, characters, businesses, organizations, places, events and incidents either are the product of the author's imagination or are used fictitiously. Any resemblance to actual persons, living or dead, events, or locales is entirely coincidental.

CHAPTER 1

Early Mornings

A few months passed as Karen and Jonny settled into their life in Spain; getting used to the new surroundings was easy for Jonny, but Karen found it hard to leave her family behind and there were many nights she spent crying wanting to go home. She knew though that it would be impossible for Jonny to return to N. Ireland and to the Shankill Road, so she bottled up her feelings and kept telling herself that it would get easier as time passed.

*

Each morning I got up at 7am and went for a run along the beach, I loved this part of the day the most. As I jogged along the water's edge with the blue sky and the sun beating down on me, it was so relaxing and I knew I was where I wanted to be in life. As I got to the end of the beach, I stopped to catch my breath; I sat on a rock at the water's edge and took my trainers and socks off, I dipped my feet in the water - it was cold at first but as I sat looking out over the ocean, the sun warmed me up. I felt a hand on my shoulder and it made me jump, as I looked over my shoulder there stood Karen.

"Morning gorgeous, I thought I would join you for a walk," Karen said.

"Jesus Karen, you give me a fright there."

"Sorry Jonny."

"It's ok, just wasn't expecting you."

Karen sat down beside me and took her trainers and socks off as well, as we walked back along the beach in the shallow water holding hands and chatting, Karen said to me, "Jonny, we have been living here a while now, we are going to have to think about getting jobs. Our money isn't going to last forever."

"I know Karen I have been thinking about that as well, the only thing I have experience for is working behind a bar, but the wages wouldn't be enough, do you think we could run our own bar?"

"I don't know Jonny, where would you have it, here or in Benidorm?"

"It would have to be Benidorm as there would be more chance of it working, the amount of stag and hen parties that go would be enough to keep it busy."

"So how do we would go about it then?"

"I don't know Karen, after breakfast we will take a drive up and take a look around to see if there are any bars for sale or lease."

As we sat eating breakfast on the veranda of our 3 bedroom semi-detached house, I looked around.

"You know Karen, I love living here, I could only have dreamt of being here with you and I know no matter what we go to do we will make a success of it. When we go up to Benidorm we need to think of where the Bar is going to be, we really need it in a central location. We'll also need a theme for it and think about what to call it."

"I know Jonny, I am really excited about us running our own Bar, but what about staff? We couldn't work all the hours ourselves."

"We will have to for a while until we get it up and running, but let's not get ahead of ourselves, we need to find a bar for sale that we can afford."

"How much can we afford Jonny?"

"I reckon if we could pick a place up for 20 grand then we could have 10 grand to get it up and running and change the inside a bit. It would be even better if we could lease a place for a while with a chance to buy, but we won't know until we get up there."

"Come on, we will head there now, I'm that excited I can't wait any longer."

"Ok, let's get this tided up before we leave."

And at that we washed the dishes and tided up the house.

As we locked up the front door I held Karen's hand, as we walked to the car I said, "You know Karen this is a big step for us both, are you sure you want to do this?"

"Yes Jonny, I would love to give it a go, what's the

worst could happen?"

"Apart from lose about 30 grand, then nothing."

"I know Jonny, are we mad?"

"Sure, if you don't try these things you will never know."

At that Karen squeezed my hand that little bit tighter and then we got into the car.

As we drove up the coast with the windows down and the music pumping, life couldn't get any better.

After about 20 minutes we arrived in Benidorm; we drove around a while but couldn't see any bars for sale so we decided to park the car and go and ask in an estate agent if they knew of any.

As we walked round the streets I noticed a few of the bars that I had been in when Billy and his mates took me, it made me smile. I realised then that I knew what sort of bar I wanted and that made me more determined to find the right one.

"Jonny, who could we ask if there are any for sale?"

"I'm not sure Karen, I can't even see an estate agency, come on, we will ask in here."

As I ushered Karen into a bar, we were greeted by a dark haired girl.

"Are you in for lunch?"

"Not exactly," I replied. "We are looking for a bit of information."

The girl was quite attractive, short dark hair, swarthy skin, I was surprised when she spoke as she sounded like she was from N. Ireland but she looked Spanish.

"Oh right, how can I help you?"

"We are wanting to know if there are any estate agents round here?"

"Are you looking to buy a holiday home?"

"No, we already live just up the coast a bit, we are looking to buy or lease a bar and we don't know how to go about it."

The girl stood there in silence, it was a bit awkward. You know those moments when nothing is said and everyone looks at each other waiting for someone to speak? Well that was this moment.

Karen spoke up, "Do you know of any for sale?"

"Can you take a seat, you might be what I have been hoping for."

"What do you mean?" I asked.

"My boss is looking to retire, he wants to lease this place and don't tell him I told you but he has been trying to lease it now for a year and if he doesn't get it leased by the end of the month then he is closing it. I will be out of a job as well as my flat above here and I will have to go home to Bangor."

"I knew you were from N. Ireland," I replied. "How long have you been out here? Sorry, I'm Jonny and this is Karen," I said, as I shook her hand she introduced herself as Paula.

"I have been out here 5 years now and I love it apart from my boss being hard to work for, but I love the place and would be devastated to have to leave."

"Is it just he is retiring or is the place not doing well?" I asked.

"It's a bit of both to be honest, he has no interest anymore; when I first started here we were one of the busiest bars in Benidorm, but he just let the place go and let his standards slide. To be honest, it's going to close so you might be coming in at the right time."

"Can we take a walk around the place to get a feel for it?"

"Yeah that will be fine. I tell you what, I will ring my boss and tell him you're here, it will probably take him about half an hour to come down but it will give you a chance to look around."

"That's perfect, Paula, can I ask you something?"

"Yes sure Jonny, what is it?"

"How many staff work here now?"

"You're looking at the staff Jonny, I run the Bar and my Boss does the food, badly I may add."

"Oh dear Paula, that's not good."

"I know Jonny, that's why I think you could name your price."

"What was he asking for to buy it?"

"He won't sell, he just wants to lease it and he was looking 500 euro a week but I'm sure you could beat him down a bit."

"That's good to know Paula, thanks for the info."

At that Paula walked towards the bar, dialling on her mobile phone.

"Well that was a stroke of luck Karen, what do you

think?"

"I don't know Jonny, Paula says it's going under."

"But that will help us get it at the right price," I replied.

"Would you keep Paula on?" Karen asked

"If we can get the lease down a bit then yeah, she would be perfect as she would know all the suppliers."

"Suppose so Jonny, it still seems too good to be true to be honest."

"Come on and we will take a look around."

CHAPTER 2

Fixtures And Fittings

As we walked around the bar, I counted the tables and chairs which were a bit tatty looking to be honest, I wouldn't want to sit and have lunch at them. In total there was 20 tables and 80 chairs, looking at the layout I said to Karen, "You could definitely make the layout better and fit a few more tables in which would put more bums on seats."

"Yeah Jonny, that's all well and good but I think the problem is getting any bums on seats." As Karen looked at her watch she said, "It's now 12.30 and we are the only ones here."

"Suppose you're right Karen, but I mean to change that we have to stay positive."

As we walked to the end of the bar I saw that there was a curtain across, I pulled it open just as Paula came walking over. She said, "Carlos will be here shortly, this used to be a stage area but we haven't had any entertainment on in absolutely ages."

My eyes widened as I looked at the size of the area which wasn't being used, you could fit a five piece band on really comfortably and that would be a great way to make this place a success. It was in a bit of a state but after a lick of paint and a good scrub, it would be useable.

I turned to Paula and said, "Is there any other parts of the bar hidden away like this?"

She replied, "Well there is a back room but it is only used as a store room now."

"Can we see it Paula?"

"Yes of course you can," she said as she walked over to the other side of the bar and pulled back a folding screen.

She was right, it was full of broken chairs and tables and boxes of stuff, there were crates of beer and tins of *Coke* as well. I looked at Karen and said, "This is looking promising, we should get this side opened up as well."

"Slow down Jonny, you are talking like you have already decided what we are doing, we need to speak with the owner first before we decide anything."

"I know Karen, it's the first place we have looked at but it feels right and look outside, it is in a really good spot – only 5 minutes from the beach. We could get people in at lunch time for food and then at night put a good group on and the people will come."

Just at that a big Jeep pulled up outside and an elderly looking man got out, he smiled as he walked over to the bar. When he was about 10 feet away, he put his hand out and said in a broken English accent,

"Hola I am Carlos, I believe you are interested in my bar?"

I put my hand out and shook Carlos' hand, "I am Jonny and this is Karen, it was pure luck that we came into your bar, Paula tells me you want to lease the place?"

"I do Jonny but let's not get ahead of ourselves, we will have lunch first."

At that Carlos asked Paula, "Can you bring some lunch out for us please?"

Paula looked at Karen and me, "What would you like?"

I looked at Karen, she replied, "I don't know Paula, a wee sandwich would do."

Carlos spoke up, "Not at all Karen, we do a great burger and chips here, we will have 3 of them Paula."

Karen went a wee bit red and I replied, "Yeah, that's fine Carlos."

He ushered us over to a table by the window and we sat down.

"Do you know anything about running a bar Jonny?"

"Yes Carlos I actually do, I worked in a bar for a few years back home."

"Oh and where is home Jonny?"

"Shankill Road in Belfast."

"Oh right," Carlos replied as he dropped his head.

"What's wrong with the Shankill Road Carlos?"

"Jonny, don't take offence, but I find it hard to

trust anyone from Ireland."

"That's where I will stop you there Carlos, I am a man of my word and it works both ways, how do I know I can trust you?"

Carlos looked at me hard and said, "So we will have to trust each other then?"

"No Carlos, all you need to trust is the colour of my money and I assure you I won't let you down. First though, I need to know more about the business end and what money is coming in."

Just at that Paula came out with our burger and chips it looked lovely.

"Thanks Paula," Karen said as Paula handed her the plate.

I said, "Thanks Paula, this looks lovely."

"No worries, enjoy, would you like any sauces?" Paula replied.

"Red sauce would be perfect and some vinegar please," I answered.

Carlos spoke up, "Would you like something to drink?"

"I could murder a pint Carlos, what would you like Karen?"

"Just a *Diet Coke* for me please."

Carlos walked over to the bar and poured our drinks, I turned to Karen and said, "Well what do you think?"

Karen replied, "The burger is nice but the chips are a bit hard."

"No you bloody header, the bar?" I laughed and Karen laughed as well.

"Oh right, Jonny this place is perfect, I could see us working here but don't show Carlos we are too eager to get it, we need to get it at the right money."

"Jesus Karen, you sounded like Billy there, I know but when I decide I want something I can't hide my emotions."

"You will have to, these Spaniards will screw us for money Jonny so play it cool."

Carlos came walking over with our drinks just as Paula came back with the vinegar and sauce.

"There you go Jonny, that is the best pint you will get in Benidorm," he handed me the pint and I took a big drink of it and to be fair, it wasn't bad.

"Not bad, thanks very much."

We finished our lunch and then he showed us round the rest of the bar, the toilets were not great and would have to be replaced. Karen couldn't even go into the gents' toilet, the smell was enough for her and she went outside for air which gave me a chance to talk money with him.

"So Carlos, the big question is, how much do you need a month for this place?"

He put his hand up to his chin and replied, "Well Jonny that is the magic question, so you want the place then?"

"It depends on the money Carlos and how long you will lease it to me and if you will eventually sell it to me?"

"Sit down Jonny and we will discuss the details." He looked over to Karen who was now looking a bit better after getting fresh air, "Karen come and sit down and join us."

Karen walked over and sat beside me holding my hand under the table, I caught a whiff of her perfume and looked at her and smiled. She was beaming, I think she wanted this placed as much as I did.

"Well Jonny, I would need to get 600 euro a week and I would review that after 2 years."

Karen kicked me under the table, we both knew what Paula had told us and Karen was right, he was trying to screw us. I spoke up, "Carlos that's a bit much for a bar that isn't busy, we wouldn't be able to go up to that much."

"Then we can't do business Jonny," he replied.

I looked at Karen and then looked back at Carlos and said, "Sorry, we have wasted your time then mate," and I took Karen by the hand and stood up.

Just at that Paula came over and started speaking really angrily in Spanish at him, they both got into an argument. Karen and I just stood there, it was really awkward as Paula ripped into him, who gave as good as he got. It must have went on for a good 5 minutes but when it did eventually finish, Carlos turned to me and said, "Sit down again Jonny, I think we will be able to do business."

I looked at Karen and we both sat down, I looked at Paula and said, "Paula, can you sit down as well as this involves you too."

She looked at Carlos who said, "Sit down." He

really was a typical Spaniard, quite aggressive in the way he spoke and I think Paula really wanted us to take the bar over so she sat down and smiled at us both.

"Carlos, I will make you an offer but you have to hear me out first."

"Ok, what do you want to say?"

Looking at him, he had such a frown on his face, I think he knew what was coming.

"Your Bar is lovely and well laid out in a good location but it is run down and would need a lot of money pumped into it to make it work. We are willing to do that but I would need a lease that is going to be realistic to the standard it is in now and if it does work I would want to buy it at its market value which it is priced at today and that's the only deal I would be willing to do."

He sat in silence, it was an eternity before he spoke, "So what would you be offering Jonny?"

"I will give you 1000 euro up front as a good will gesture and then 400 euro a week for 1 year and then if we are still in business, I will pay you 500 euro a week for a further 3 years."

He stood up and started walking to the bar speaking in Spanish, we hadn't a clue what he was saying but the look on Paula's face said it all, she was smiling so I knew he was going to take the deal.

I looked over at Carlos who was behind the bar and had 3 glasses set on the bar and he was pouring some type of shot into them, he was still speaking in Spanish when he walked back over he set the drinks on the table and then handed both Karen and I one each.

"So we have a deal then?" he said with a really angry look on his face.

"No not yet," I said as I sat my drink down. Karen looked confused, as I looked at her I said, "Carlos, can you pour Paula a drink as well as she is part of the deal too." I looked at Paula and said, "We would like you to stay Paula if you will have us as bosses?"

She smiled as Carlos got up and again muttering in Spanish, he walked to the bar and poured Paula a drink, he returned as Paula said, "I would love to Jonny, thank you."

"No Paula, thank you."

We all chinked glasses and drank our drink and the deal was sealed.

CHAPTER 3

Buffaloes

We agreed the deal and the hand over was to be the following week when Carlos got the appropriate paper work drawn up. I had to pay for the solicitor which was 300 euros, but I didn't mind as I was glad the deal was done and we were turning our dream into a reality.

On the drive up home we were buzzing, ideas were flying, Karen said to me, "Jonny, I can't believe what we have just done, you are bonkers, I thought we were just going up to look."

"Well Karen, you got to strike while the iron is hot and if you don't take a chance in life you will never know what you can achieve."

"Look at you wee Jonny from the Shankill Road, you are quite the philosopher and quite the business man."

We both laughed and sang along to the song on

the radio.

Just as we arrived home, my phone rang, it was Paula.

"Hi Jonny, can you talk?"

"Yes Paula, what's up?"

"I need to meet you and Karen before you sign any contracts with Carlos."

Paula sounded worried which I didn't like, "What's wrong Paula? You sound worried."

"Nothing's wrong Jonny, I just need to know where I stand when you take over."

"Oh right Paula, that's fine, would tomorrow suit you?"

"Yes Jonny, that would be perfect, it's my day off so any time would suit."

"What about 11 o'clock? Where do you want to meet?"

"Can you meet me along the promenade? There is a bar called Tiki Beach, do you know it?"

"Yes Paula, I know where that is, we will meet you at 11."

"Ok Jonny, see you then."

And at that Paula hung up.

"What's wrong with Paula?" Karen asked.

"Nothing love, she just wants to discuss her job with us."

"Oh right, that's fine," Karen replied.

We decided to spend the rest of the afternoon

round at the communal pool, which was really nice; it had palm trees and a lot of grass around a huge pool with some sunbeds scattered round, it was for everyone who lived in our block of houses and it was a great opportunity to meet the neighbours and get to know people who lived here all year round.

We lifted our towels and the beach bag which already had sun cream and our sun glasses in, it was a short walk just around the corner and we had our own key to open the gate to get to the pool area.

There were only a few people sitting round the pool, I spotted the big German and his wife who could only speak broken English, I think you call him Otto but I'm not sure as we had only met them a couple of times. He was a monster of a man, about 6 foot 6 inches and as wide as he was tall. His wife was the complete opposite, lightly made up dark hair and a very quiet women, you called her Helga and they were both in their early 60s, they'd retired to live in a warmer climate.

"Good afternoon Otto, how are you?" I said as we walked towards the pool area.

"Ok Jonny, how is you?"

"Not too bad, the weather is beautiful as usual."

"It is so nice here and the pool is nice to quickly cool off."

"It is Otto, that's where I am going now to cool off."

Karen and Helga just smiled at each other as Helga really struggled with her English and there was no chance of Karen or me even trying to speak German.

We got two sun beds right beside the pool, Karen absolutely loved sun bathing and she suited the nice glow she had now with her tan. I loved the sun as well and since going away with Billy for the weekend, I knew this is where I wanted to be.

I walked over to the pool's edge and dove straight in, the glistening water instantly cooled me down and I swam under water for a few seconds and surfaced half way across the pool. It was so refreshing and to have this as our private pool was a dream come true.

I swam a couple of lengths and then got out to lie on the sunbed next to Karen, I didn't even have to dry off as the warm sun dried me in a few minutes. It was so relaxing just lying there I fell asleep for a while, as did Karen.

The next day we went to meet Paula, walking down the promenade was just breath taking, the amount of people just out walking and enjoying the beautiful weather was fantastic. Everyone we passed looked so happy and relaxed and the view out over the ocean, seeing some people on jet skis and a couple of nice yachts sail by, made us realise how lucky we were living in Spain and on the verge of getting our own bar.

As we walked past Tiki Beach bar we heard Paula call us, we turned to face her and she stood there with a huge grin on her face.

"Hi Karen, hi Jonny, I'm glad you could meet me."

"No worries Paula, would you like to go for a walk or go in and sit down?" I said as I pointed to a free table in the bar.

"Could we sit down, we have a bit to discuss?"

"Yeah sure," I replied as we walked over to the table.

"Would you like a drink Karen and Paula?" I asked.

"A *Diet Coke* please," Karen replied.

"Yeah, I'll have the same please," Paula replied.

I went to the bar where I stood in a queue, I looked around and then at my watch, it was 11.20am and this bar already had a half decent crowd in all having drinks with a really good atmosphere about it. I got the drinks and returned to the table where Karen and Paula were sitting chatting,

"There we go," I said as I sat the drinks down, Karen looked up and smiled.

"Paula was telling me about the bar Jonny."

"Oh, and what about it?"

"Just how about 2 years ago it would have been as busy as this place, but Carlos lost interest and stopped caring about the people that came in and it just went downhill until he just about gave up. I was really glad that you both stumbled upon it, I really think you could make a go of it."

"So do we Paula, but the big question is: are you wanting to stay on?"

"Of course I do, I am buzzing about the thought of getting it back to the way it was, I am just worried about where I live, can I still rent the flat?"

"What were your terms with Carlos?"

"He paid me 200 euro a week but took 50 euro back for the rent of the flat, so if wasn't for my tips it would have been a struggle."

I looked at Karen, she didn't know what to say but we knew that we had to keep her on if we were to make it work.

"Paula, how many hours a week did you do?"

"Probably about 60 hours a week, I only got one day off a week but I don't mind, I love working in the bar. Listen, I am going to nip to the toilet and let you and Karen talk a minute."

"Oh right, ok."

At that Paula got up and walked over to the bar.

"What do you think Karen?" I asked.

"I don't know Jonny, what do you think?"

"I think Carlos has been taking the hand out of Paula, I know she would probably be happy with the same wages but I have a real feeling if we give her a bit more respect she would be a real asset and with getting the lease down a bit, we could afford it."

"So what are you saying Jonny?"

"Pay her 250 euro a week and let her use the flat for free, but the main thing is make her manager because I think if this place takes off the way I think it will, we will need more staff. We already need someone for the kitchen and I'm sure Paula will know someone."

"Yeah, you're probably right Jonny, you know what you're doing so offer her that."

Paula came back from the toilet and sat down, "Would you like another?"

"No I'm fine, would you like one Karen?" I asked.

"No, I'm fine too."

"Paula, we would love for you to stay on so what we would like to offer you is a manager's role within the business, how do you feel about that?"

"I'm speechless Jonny, I would love to be a manager but what would I be doing?"

"Much the same as you are doing now but when we get more staff in then you would be in charge of them and their working hours, as well as running the kitchen."

"What about wages then?" she asked.

"I like the way you get straight to the point Paula, we would like to start you on 250 euro a week but with free accommodation."

Paula put her hand out, "I definitely will be staying then."

We shook hands but when Paula turned to Karen, she gave her a hug and thanked us both for the opportunity.

"I won't let you down, I promise you that, but can I gave you a bit of advice when you meet Carlos."

"Yeah Paula, what's that?"

"Make sure it's the deal that you agreed before you sign anything, he can be a nightmare when it comes to getting what he wants."

"We will Paula, I will make sure I read the contract before I sign it."

"If you don't mind, can I be there to go over it with you? If I know Carlos, it will be partly written in Spanish."

"Then that will be your first job as manager, to make sure the contract is right."

Paula was beaming from ear to ear. "Thank you Jonny, I can't wait to get started."

"We are due to sign the contact next Monday at 2pm in the bar so we will meet you then."

"That's perfect, I wondered why Carlos gave me that day off, he is definitely up to something, so it will be my final goodbye to him by making sure he doesn't take you both on."

"That's great Paula, we will see you then."

We both thanked Paula and after she left we stayed on for lunch and then had a walk around the many bars just to get a few ideas. We were also hoping it could maybe push us towards something different than the many sports bars that were there.

The next few days we were bouncing ideas off each other but what we came up with was brilliant: an American style theme with flamed grilled burgers and fries with all the trimmings for a lunch menu with about 10 different types to choose from. It would be easy to get up and running really quickly and of course a name: 'BUFFALOES' is what we were to name it, which I had thought of, with the staff all dressed up accordingly to make it look like a ranch style bar.

We had sourced out a local building firm to make the changes that we were going to need but couldn't get it started until we signed the lease, which couldn't come any quicker.

Monday came round and we sat at a table with Carlos and another man that was introduced to us as

Mateo and he was Carlos' solicitor, but we had a problem, Paula was right, some of the contract was in Spanish and there was no sign of Paula. It was quite awkward as I didn't want to sign it as god knows what I would be signing. I kept looking at my watch which now read 2.30, Carlos was getting a bit annoyed but I told him I was waiting for Paula to arrive which he didn't like. He kept talking to Mateo and raising his arms a lot so I knew something wasn't right, just as he got up from the table and I am sure he was swearing in Spanish, Paula pulled up outside in a taxi. She got out of the car with a middle aged man and walked into the bar, the man was dressed in a nice pair of trousers and shirt and tie, when they came walking over Carlos wasn't too happy. Karen nudged me under the table and I stood up, "Hi Paula, thanks for coming."

Carlos just glared at her, he really wasn't happy she was there.

"Hi Jonny, this is Peter, I wanted him to come along to meet you both and to make sure everything was above board."

I put my hand out and shook Peter's, "Thanks for coming along Peter."

"Not a problem Jonny, I'm here to help."

Carlos spoke up, "Can we just get on with it?"

"Hold on a minute mate, if you want me to lease your bar it has to be what we agreed or we don't have a deal."

"It is the deal we agreed, just sign the bloody papers," he replied quite angrily.

"Paula, can you read the Spanish parts out for me?" I asked as the look on his face could tell a thousand words.

Paula started reading and when she got to the part of buying the bar after 2 years at today's market price, we saw that this was where he was going to take us on. He really was a snake in the grass and he knew what he was doing. He was never going to sell the bar but make the lease extortionate and so take it back, but what he didn't realise was that I wasn't stupid and after about 30 minutes of arguing and changing the agreement, we finally made the deal that we wanted and I signed it and gave him the 1000 euros. He handed me the keys and wished us good luck and he and his solicitor left.

The feeling of owning my own bar was amazing. Paula then explained who Peter was, he was a chef who worked for a few years in one of the other bars but was wanting a new challenge and was willing to work within our budget. So in one day we had got our bar and staff which could make it work. Peter knew all the local suppliers and with Paula's connections we were able to get things put in place really quickly and within 2 weeks we were ready for opening night.

CHAPTER 4

Opening Night

Over the past 2 weeks we redecorated the whole place, new toilets were put in and we were able to buff the wooden floor down and it came up like new. We bought all new tables and chairs and Peter designed the menu to even include steaks that you cooked yourself on a hot stone at your own table, I thought it was a super idea and something really different. I think giving Paula and Peter a bit of a free run really got them motivated to make the place special and it was them alone that did the advertising and leaflet drops in the 2 weeks that we had to get the place open.

And it had arrived, the grand opening of Buffaloes. I got a load of cheap champagne and everyone that came in got a glass, even the local newspaper sent a photographer down to take photos which Peter organised. It felt really special when Karen cut the ribbon that was across the front doors and we were open.

We had two guys playing country music and they were really good, all the old favourites, even Kenny Rodgers got a spin which made me smile.

We didn't serve food, we just wanted a party atmosphere and what a party we had, both Paula and myself never left the bar and Karen put herself between the bar and helping Peter clear tables, it was packed. Karen designed a cocktail menu which went down well and by the end of the night we were absolutely wrecked. The group had finished at 12, we thought it would have slowed down but no, everyone there was still parting and it was 2am when the last customers left.

As I locked the doors and poured us all a well-deserved drink, we sat round a table and chatted.

"That was some night."

"I know Jonny, we never stopped all night," Karen replied.

"That was brilliant, I haven't been as busy in ages," Paula said.

"The only problem we have now is that we've got to keep it going."

"We will Jonny, everyone will be talking about Buffaloes, I think the only problem you're going to have is we need more staff," Peter asked.

"I know Peter but we will give it a week to see if we are still as busy, I have a few ideas in mind but we definitely will need another 2 or 3. Paula, that's your department, would you know anyone that would be interested in working here?"

"You are having a laugh Jonny, they will be beating

your door down to get a job here if tonight is anything to go by. You will be able to pick and choose."

"Peter, let's see how your new menu goes tomorrow and then over the next couple of days we will be able to judge it better."

"Jonny I am shattered, can we lock up and head home? Tomorrow will be another big day."

"Yeah Karen, you're right."

As we finished our drinks, Peter said his goodnights and said he would be in for 10am to get the prep done.

"Jonny, if you and Karen want to shoot on I will lock up, I don't mind."

"Brilliant Paula, that's great."

I lifted the takings and both Karen and I left for home.

Karen fell asleep on the way home in the car, when we got home she went straight to bed. I was still on a high and decided to count the takings and we lifted nearly 3000 euro which was superb, I only expected about half that but it was the start we needed. It worried me a bit about having that sort of money in the house as this was only the first night, so I was going to need a safe put in here and probably in the bar as well.

The next morning, even though I only had about 5 hours' sleep, I was up early. I needed to get things done and told Karen I would be back at 11.30 to pick her up to start work in Buffaloes.

I drove down to the bar and was there for about 9.30am. Paula was already up and cleaning the bar, getting the glasses washed, as I walked in I said, "Morning Paula, are you not tired?"

"No Jonny, I'm fine, I needed to get the bar sorted. I have made you a drinks order as well, we have ran out of a few things."

Paula was superb, she really knew the ropes and what needed to be done which took the pressure off me a bit. I placed the order just as Peter arrived, he smiled and walked straight in to the kitchen, after the phone call I followed him in.

"Morning Peter, what do you need?"

"Nothing Jonny, I have placed an order and it will be here in 30 minutes so it's all good."

This was too good to be true, Peter and Paula were brilliant, it gave me a chance to go and order two safes and the guy was able to fit the one in the bar that afternoon. Everything was going well.

I drove back up home to pick Karen up and on the way back to the bar she said to me, "Jonny, I have been thinking about a theme."

"Sure, we have a theme Karen, American style country."

"No, you don't know what I mean, not for during the day, I really think our bar should go all out on the party theme."

"Sounds good, what do you have in mind?"

As we drove down the motorway I was that engrossed in what Karen was saying I didn't notice a car pull out in front of me until the last minute. I hit the brakes and swerved to avoid an accident, grabbing the steering wheel I shouted, "Fuck, what are you doing, dick head?" Karen was screaming. I got in the way of a coach that was coming up at pace, I was able to swerve across another lane to avoid the bus who now had hit his brakes and had his lights flashing and horn blasting. He also swerved to miss me but clipped the car that had pulled out in front of me, as I looked over my left shoulder the bus was now into the side of the other car, pushing him sideways up the road. When I finally stopped, the whole road was a mess, the bus had really thumped the other car which had flipped a few times, landing on its roof. Karen was crying as I looked at her in total shock, I reassured her that we were ok before I got out to see if anyone was hurt. Two other cars had been caught up in the accident which had closed most of the road, one lane was just open so it didn't take long for a lot of traffic to create a jam. I walked towards the bus which was across two lanes and the driver was already out.

"Are you ok mate?" I asked as the Spanish driver was shouting, waving his arms in the air.

I got to the front of the bus and it was then that the realization of what had happened hit me. I looked up the road and there was a white BMW in bits, the whole road was scattered with debris from the car. As I walked closer, the bus driver had calmed down, he also saw the mess of the car and we both knew someone was in trouble, my heart sank as I walked past a child's car seat and teddy bear lying in the road. As I looked up I could see smoke starting to rise from the car, I looked at the bus driver, he went silent and turned pale. Even though we couldn't understand each other, we both knew that this was bad and we had to act quickly, I ran towards the car where the driver was lying upside down still belted into his seat. I quickly looked inside the rest of the car to find it empty, I ran round to the driver's side, the smoke was starting to get thick as I reached in trying to release the man from his seatbelt, but it wouldn't release. I started shouting, "Help, someone help me, I can't get him out."

I pulled and pulled at the seat belt, the smoke was now getting over powering and then it happened.

Flames started rising from the engine, my heart was racing, I stood up and looked back towards the bus where the driver and some other people were standing. I was screaming for help but I couldn't hear myself and got no reaction from the people standing watching. I could see Karen, she was in a state, we looked at each other and she was shouting something but I couldn't hear, everything was silent. I turned back to the car where the flames had really taken hold, the whole front of the car was engulfed and the man was now awake and struggling to break free. I don't know what came over me but I reached into the car and ripped the seat belt from the floor and I grabbed the man and trailed him from the now balls of flames that had engulfed the whole motor. I got him about 10 feet from the car when it exploded and blew me off my feet.

The next I knew I was laying at the side of the road with Karen beside me, I was breathing really quickly. An ambulance pulled up as Karen said to me, "Jonny are you ok, are you hurt?"

I looked at her, she had tears running down her cheeks, she held my hand, I went to sit up she said, "Jonny don't, just stay where you are, let the medics take a look at you."

I answered, "Karen I am fine, I'm not hurt."

I sat up, I didn't even have an ache or a pain, I got to my feet and looked round at what had happened. Karen threw her arms around me, she was crying, she said through her sobs, "Jonny you should have ran, you could have been killed." She squeezed me really tightly, we held each other for a couple of minutes and then one of the medics tapped me on the shoulder.

"Excuse me senior, I need to take a look at you, can you walk to the back of the ambulance?"

I let go of Karen and said, "Yeah sure, but I am ok."

"I will be the judge of that, senior."

I followed him to the back of the ambulance, as I walked over I saw two other medics deal with the man that I had pulled free. He was awake but he lay on the ground not moving, we exchanged a glance as I walked past him and he sort of gave a smile, I smiled back. I reached the back of the ambulance, the medic said to me, "Can you take a seat here senior?" as he pointed inside the ambulance.

I stepped up into the back of it and it brought back bad memories, but I sat down and let the medic get on with his checks. It took about 10 minutes but I had escaped with just a minor burn on my right forearm and I thanked him as he bandaged me up.

The police had arrived and as I looked over, the bus driver was pointing over to me as he spoke to one of them. I thought to myself, *'Oh dear, here we go.'* One of the officers came over and started taking my details, I told him what had happened and the bus driver collaborated my version of the events that had happened and after about half an hour we were allowed to leave.

I walked over to the back of the ambulance where the injured man was now laid.

I asked the medic, "Is it ok if I speak to him?"

He replied, "Yes senior."

I stepped in, the man was strapped up, he was fully conscious. I asked him, "Are you ok mate?"

He replied, "I am so sorry for what happened, I am glad you are not hurt."

"Wow, hold on, it was an accident you can't blame yourself."

"I can and I will, I am fully responsible for what happened and I am lucky to be alive, you don't know what this means, thank you so much."

"I didn't do anything that no one else would have done, there is no thanks needed."

"What's your name?"

"Jonny Andrews, I own Buffaloes bar in Benidorm."

"Listen Jonny, when I get sorted I am going to come and see you and thank you properly."

"I told you, you don't need to thank me but call in for lunch sometime."

"I will Jonny."

My phone started ringing as I got back out of the ambulance, it was Paula.

"Jonny, where are you? We are about to open up."

"Sorry Paula we got caught up in an accident but we will be there shortly," I replied as I walked towards Karen who I think was still in shock at what had happened.

"Are you ok Karen?"

"I am now Jonny, but we could have been killed."

"I know Karen but we weren't and we need to get to the bar."

"There is no way Jonny you can work today after what has happened."

"Karen, all the things that have happened in my life, today was nothing, we will be fine, are you ok to work?"

"I don't know Jonny, but we need to go and get it open anyway."

We got into our car and drove the short journey into the town and to the bar.

CHAPTER 5

A Big Surprise

Paula was glad to see us as she had already opened up and had about 10 people in for lunch. Peter was working away in the kitchen getting the orders ready so we had no time to explain what had happened, we both just got stuck into serving the customers. I looked at my watch, it was now near 2pm and the bar was in full flow. Paula was busy bringing the orders out of the kitchen and they looked lovely, it made me feel hungry but we had no time to eat, the place was packing up and it made me realise that we definitely needed more staff. When I got a chance, I swiped a few chips and shoved them in my mouth but that just made me even more hungry. As I was coming back out of the kitchen, Paula was coming in. "Paula, would you know anyone who could come and work today? We are really snowed under and to be honest, we could do with another two."

"Actually Jonny I will make a phone call, I might

be able to get a couple of mates to help out."

"Brilliant Paula."

I looked over at Karen, she was really busy, every table was full and there was a great atmosphere about the place, we were flying. Peter had the kitchen running like clockwork, Paula and Karen taking and giving out orders and clearing tables and I was behind the bar serving the drinks and taking the money. It wasn't long before a fella and girl came up to the bar and said that Paula had phoned them and said that there might be a job for them. The fella was in his twenties, he was quite tall and dark haired, he dressed really smart with a dark coloured pair of jeans and a white muscle top, he looked the part with his slick backed black hair and a tan. The girl was good looking as well, she also had a pair of jeans on and nice black top, she had dark hair as well but what struck me about her was that she smelt lovely, her perfume was really strong, she was also in her twenties. I looked at the both of them and asked, "Have you both done bar work before?"

The guy answered, "Yeah mate, we have worked in various bars over the last few years."

"What are your names?" I asked as Karen came walking over.

"Jonny, I am snowed under, you are going to have to give me a hand."

I looked at Karen, she looked exhausted, I think the morning's incident was starting to take a toll on her.

"I know love, we are really busy, I will be with you in a minute."

The girl introduced herself to Karen as Julie and turned to me and said, "You must be Jonny, this is a busy bar, you really need to give us a chance to let you see how we work and then decide after today if you want to give us a job."

"Julie is right Jonny, I am Dylan and looking around your bar we haven't got time to discuss the details, we need to get on with getting these customers served and kept happy."

I shook both their hands and said, "If Paula says you both are right for the bar then the only thing to do is to discuss wages."

"We will discuss that tomorrow Jonny, let's get stuck in and make this place the best bar in Benidorm."

At that they both started taking drinks orders and clearing tables, I went behind the bar and I swear I couldn't even come up for air, it was frantic. In those three hours we never stopped, it wasn't till after 5pm that it started slowing down and we were able to get something to eat ourselves and take a bit of a break.

At 6pm I closed the doors for 45 minutes to get the place cleaned up and get the bar restocked, as I just closed the doors I looked over to where Karen was sitting, she looked wrecked. I walked over and sat beside her, I put my arm round her and gave her a kiss on the cheek. "Are you ok love?"

She looked round, "Jonny I am shattered, I can hardly keep my eyes open."

"Then its home for you."

At that Paula came over, "Karen, why don't you go up to my flat and get your head down for a couple of hours and then help out later when we get busy again?"

"That would be great," Karen replied as she looked at me. "Jonny would you mind if I went for a couple of hours?"

"Wise up Karen, of course I don't mind, away you go, I will come up and get you if we need you."

Karen leant over and gave me a kiss and said, "Ok love, I will see you later."

She left and went up to Paula's flat leaving the five of us to get ready to open up again.

At 6.45 we opened up, a few people started arriving, this was our first night we were serving food and Peter's idea of cook your own steak seemed to be a winner. I was amazed at the way he had it set up, he brought down a red hot slab of stone and the raw meat, the first time it was set up I couldn't trail myself away from the customers' table, the smell of the steak cooking was lovely and he even let them cook their own onions which put me over the edge, my stomach thought my throat was cut. It smelt fabulous and it looked as good as it smelt. Peter gave the customers a few choices of sides, chunky chips, sweet chilli fries, mashed potatoes and my favourite, champ. As soon as the smell drifted round the bar the orders for steaks started coming in thick and fast it was hard to keep up with the demand but we managed to get everyone served and the turnaround of customers was really quick. We did nearly 80 covers in under 3 hours. At 9 o'clock the food stopped and the guy arrived that I had hired for the entertainment, he introduced himself and got set up, he sat in the middle of the stage on a stool with a guitar and started singing. He had the place buzzing and singing along to his tunes. A hen party then arrived, there were about 15 women of various ages from some young ones at about 18 to a couple of grannies aged about 70. One of the girls came up to the bar to get drinks.

"Hi, do you have a cocktail menu?"

"Yeah, hold on a second," I replied as I reached the menu from the side of the till. Karen's timing couldn't have came any better as when she walked in through the front door, a stag party walked in too - about 10 fellas all dressed in sailor uniforms and with the girls all dressed in swim suits, it was a party waiting to happen.

Karen walked behind the bar, she looked at me. "Hi Gorgeous, have you missed me?"

She was beaming, I answered her, "I have, did you enjoy your sleep?"

"Yeah love, I did, I really needed it."

She turned to the girl as she lifted her head from the drinks menu.

"Can we have 5 jugs of sex on the beach please and 15 glasses?"

One of the guys that came in was standing beside her, "That's a lot of sex you're having there."

"Easy on son, you don't know what you're getting into," the girl replied, I just looked at him I knew what was coming and I couldn't help but laugh as he replied.

"Play your cards right love and it could be you, sexy."

We all stood there laughing, this was going to be a mad night.

Karen handed the girl a tray of glasses and had the jugs poured in a few minutes. I served the fella and they were all on vodka shots, they were some drinkers as round after round was taken away from the bar.

By 10 o'clock it was packed, Paula, Julie and Dylan were now taking drinks orders leaving Karen, Peter and myself behind the bar. The crack was brilliant and the night flew by; at 12.30am it started slowing down as the entertainment finished at 12, I was able to let Peter, Dylan and Julie head on home. We closed the bar at 2am after the final customers moved on to the clubs and putting that bolt across the front door was a huge relief as our first full day of opening with food was a success.

Karen, Paula and I sat round a table and had a drink, we talked about maybe doing something different entertainment wise and Karen came up with a super idea which we would organise for that Saturday night.

I lifted the takings and put them into my safe in the office and locked up and set the alarms. Paula said goodnight and went on up to her flat and Karen and I drove home, it only took us about 20 minutes and we fell into bed, exhausted.

The next few days were much the same, we were as busy as the first day and when Saturday came round I was really looking forward to that night's entertainment. Karen had it all organised, she had four guys and four girls arranged to be in the bar for 10.30, when we were at our most busy. The guys were dressed in just ripped jeans and cowboy boots with gun holsters on and fake guns that shot caps and the girls had bikinis on and cowboy boots with gun holsters that carried bottles of vodka. When they walked in from the kitchen the DJ played a Blues Brother song, *'Raw Hide'*, the place went mad as the guys and girls got up on the bar and started dancing to it. The bar was bouncing, as the fellas in the bar were ogling the 4 girls up on the bar the girls poured vodka into their mouths and the girls in the bar couldn't keep their hands off the fellas up on the bar. They were all really good looking and muscly as well; as the song finished, the guys shot their guns in the air and the place went wild, they got off the bar and just filtered into the now packed floor. As I looked over the place, it was heaving, everyone was having a super night and the till never stopped. The punters were spending money hand over fist, even a couple of the entertainment mucked in to serve for a while, we were that busy and it was the usual 2pm before we got closed up.

As we all sat round a couple of tables I ordered pizza in for everyone and we sat chatting about that night's entertainment and it was agreed we would have that set on from Thursday through to Sunday. It was what we needed to stand out from the rest of the bars in Benidorm.

The next few weeks went by in a flash and we were well established now with a big pull of the crowds that made Benidorm the buzzing place to party. I now had ten staff that shared the hours, which enabled Karen and me to spend more quality time together.

Buffaloes was earning big money now and we were able to pay the staff a good wage which was Karen's idea. It was the right thing to do as our team worked well together and everyone was happy and then in turn the customers were happy, and most importantly, so was my bank balance.

It was a Sunday morning and Karen and I had the day off, we decided to take a drive down the coast and spend the day in a place called Quadamar. The beach was stunning, about 3 miles long and golden sands, there was only about 3 hotels on it and a couple of restaurants and bars, I parked the car and we lifted our towels and beach bag out of the boot.

As we walked down the rickety wooden pathway to the beach we held hands and chatted.

"Has everything turned out the way you wanted Jonny?"

I looked at Karen and smiled, "Yes Karen, it is everything I have dreamed of, everything has worked out for us."

"I know Jonny, we have been here now 10 months and I feel just the same as the first day we arrived, it really is a nice life."

As we walked onto the warm golden sand of the beach, we removed our trainers and socks. The feeling of the warm sand in between my toes was just so relaxing, the view in both directions was breath taking, it was a short walk to the water's edge where the small waves lapped at our feet. We held hands and walked up the beach, as we walked numerous people passed us of various ages and it was just lovely to smile or say good morning on such a beautiful day.

We were so in love and living in such a lovely climate made it even nicer.

"Should we set our towels down here?" I said to Karen as I pointed to a patch of sand just in front of a small beach side café near the water's edge.

"Yeah Jonny, this would be fine."

As Karen laid down our two towels I said, "I'm going for a swim if you fancy it?"

"No Jonny, you work away, maybe later." Karen started taking her shorts and t-shirt off and lay down on one of the towels. She lifted out her book that she was reading and a pair of sun glasses, she said, "I'm fine here, I want to read my Jackie Collins book, it's getting really good. I think one of the characters in it is Tom Jones, the way she describes him it has to be him, he is having sex with everyone."

"Enough said Karen, you enjoy, I'm away for a dip," I laughed as I turned to walk to the water's edge and Karen just put the book up to her face and started reading.

I stood for a minute with just my feet in the water and it wasn't the warmest, I looked down towards my feet and as the water was lapping round my ankles I noticed the scars on my knees from being kneecapped. They had faded a bit but it was a chilling reminder of a life I used to live. I walked out into the cool water and as I got deeper, the colder it got, I didn't have the courage to just dive in which probably was the right option. When the water was over my knees, the waves were a bit bigger now and every time they hit my balls it took my breath away and I squealed like a girl. There was no other option but just to go for it and dive under, so I did.

The cold water was so refreshing as I swam under, it was pretty clear and I could see about 6 feet in any direction. I was only under for a few seconds but in those seconds it was so quiet and peaceful, I noticed a small school of fish swim by and I stopped as they did. I had never seen this before, the only fish I had seen was the battered kind that came with chips and I was amazed as they all swam in sync and just disappeared into the ocean and didn't even notice me.

As I surfaced to the top, I stood up and the salty water started burning my eyes. I coughed a bit as I spat out the salty taste in my mouth, my eyes were on fire now and I rubbed them which didn't help as my hands were wet with the water. It just made them worse, I couldn't see as I stumbled towards the water's edge rubbing my eyes; in my wisdom I bent down and cupped a handful of water and threw it round my face, at first it did help but then the burning started again and it was twice as bad. I was in trouble, everything was a blur, I staggered towards where Karen was sitting, rubbing my eyes. I was in extreme pain as I stood at our two towels, I squinted at Karen and said, "Jesus Karen, my eyes are on fire, have you a bottle of water quick?"

She didn't even answer, she got up and went into her bag and handed me a bottle of water. I opened it up and splashed it over my face and in my eyes, the burning started easing and I caught my breath as I stopped panicking. Karen handed me a towel which I then used to dry my face after sitting down on the other towel.

"Excuse me senor, you are on my towel."

I took the towel away from my face and was shocked to see me sitting beside a women I didn't even know, I jumped up quicker than I sat down. I stood beside the man that had spoken to me, he was about the same height as me but quite heavy, to be honest he was a brut of a man with a big belly. He repeated himself, "What are you doing on my towel?"

I didn't know what to say, I think when I did answer him no one could have understood me. His wife stood up beside me, I turned and looked at her with my bright red face, I was dumb struck. She said, "It's ok Manuel, he couldn't see after he came out of the water, I gave him water to wash his face."

I looked over their shoulders where I noticed Karen sitting looking over in an absolute wrinkle, she was laughing really hard as she watched me squirm and try to give my apologies.

Manuel accepted my excuse and laughed with his wife as I walked towards Karen, my face was on fire. I lay down on the towel beside Karen and just wanted the sand to swallow me up.

"Well done Jonny, that was hilarious."

"You don't say Karen, I am scundered."

"Don't worry about it, it's an easy mistake to make," she said as she tried really hard not to laugh but she couldn't contain herself and just burst out laughing again. I laughed with her and the salty tears ran down my cheeks as we both just laughed it off.

We lay for a while just soaking the hot sun up and I think both off us dozed off a bit and as I dozed, my thoughts were of back home on the Shankill and Billy and the bar. It was a nice dream of all the happy times

I had back then but then I heard a voice, "Jonny, Jonny, Jonny." I looked round, I was standing behind the bar in Heather Street, I couldn't see anyone. I heard it again, "Jonny, Jonny," this time it came from behind me. I turned and Billy was standing behind me, my heart was racing as I looked at him and blood was running from his mouth and nose. I woke with a jerk, I was breathing very erraticly, my heart was pounding.

"Jonny are you ok?" Karen said, as I looked at her she knew something was wrong. "Is it the dreams again Jonny?"

I got my breathing under control and tried to calm down. "Yeah Karen, it was."

"What was it this time Jonny?"

"Karen, it was Billy, I'm really worried about him, it seemed so real."

"Jonny it was only a dream, it's not real."

"I know Karen but I need to speak with him, I haven't heard from him for a while, I need to know he is ok."

"Jonny calm down, he will be fine, give him a ring later. Let's go for lunch, I have something to tell you."

"You are probably right Karen."

We packed up our towels and headed for the beachside café where we got a table right on the beach. It was really warm so I moved our chairs out of the hot sun and under the shade of one of the umbrellas, it was a lot cooler. We ordered a couple of *Cokes* as we looked over the menu. "So what is it you have to tell me Karen?"

"It will wait till after lunch, let's order, I am starving."

The girl came down and we both ordered toasties with salad and as we sat sipping on the cold glasses of Coke I asked Karen again about what she had to tell me. She replied, "Jonny, I wanted to tell you sooner but I needed to be sure, we are going to have a baby."

I was speechless, I threw my arms around her and I squeezed her really tightly. "You're pregnant? I am going to be a daddy?"

"Yes Jonny, you are going to be a daddy."

"I can't believe it Karen, this is the best news ever, when?" I asked as I loosened my arms from around her.

"April, roundabout the 6th."

"Karen, this is fantastic." I leant over and kissed her and told her I loved her and that she has made me the happiest man alive.

The girl came back with our toasties and I ordered another couple of *Cokes*; as we sat and ate our lunch my mind was racing and there was one thing I needed to do but it would have to wait for the right time.

CHAPTER 6

The Big Question

The next few days I was walking on air, it didn't seem real but we had an appointment with the hospital to go for a scan and it was then when I heard our baby's heart beat and saw the tiny wee thing in Karen's belly that it all hit home. The doctor told us that Karen was further on than what she first thought, her due date was the 11th March which was only 8 months away, we were so excited.

"Karen I am so chuffed, it's real, we are going to have a baby."

"I know Jonny, I am chuffed as well, it feels so good knowing I am carrying our baby."

As I leant in to kiss Karen, the doctor spoke up, "Excuse me senor, I thought you both knew?"

I looked at Karen really worried, "What do you mean doctor, is there something wrong?"

"No senor, not at all, but I thought you both knew

that you were having twins."

Karen and I just looked at each other, I think we were in shock; Karen rubbed her belly.

"Twins, doctor?" she asked.

"Yes senorita, TWINS."

"Oh my god Karen, we are having Twins, that's brilliant doctor."

I leant in and hugged Karen and gave her a kiss which I think went on just that awkwardly bit too long but I didn't care, I was on cloud nine. When I stopped kissing Karen I think she was a bit embarrassed but we didn't care, our life together was going to be complete, we had everything and now 2 little babies on the way.

As soon as we got outside the hospital and into the car, Karen phoned her mum and dad and I think they were shocked at first but congratulated us both and even decided to fly out for a visit in five weeks' time which didn't give me much time to plan to marry Karen.

It was the following Wednesday that we both had the day off, we spent the day at the pool but had decided to go out for dinner so we walked down to the our local, it was called Cooper's. It was a nice wee bar that served great food, I had already told Stevie, the bar owner, what my plan was and he had things set up for me.

We sat at a nice candlelit table overlooking the ocean and I ordered a pint as I said to Karen, "What would you like to drink love?"

"A Diet Coke will do me Jonny."

Stevie took our drinks order and I said to Karen, "How you feeling today love?"

"I'm feeling great Jonny, I love being pregnant, just knowing I have our babies growing inside me feels fantastic."

"I know Karen, it's really exciting knowing we are going to be parents."

Stevie came down with our drinks.

"Are you ready to order?"

I looked at Karen, "What are you having?"

"Not sure if I want the lasagne or to go for the chicken and salad."

"You love the lasagne, why don't you get it with the chilli chunks?"

"Yeah that sounds good, what are you getting Jonny?"

"Oh, I'm getting my usual Stevie."

"Steak with chips and pepper sauce?"

"Yep, you know how I like it."

"Yes Jonny, medium with extra sauce."

I love the steaks here I hadn't the heart to tell Peter that his was second best.

Karen and I sat and chatted about her mum and dad coming over and about changing one of the rooms into a nursery for our babies, she even dropped into the mix that we would have to get a bigger car which I was wanting to do anyway. Now that our bar was well established we could afford a new car but I felt a bit sad about getting rid of my

XR2 which had so many memories, but life changes you have to just go with the flow.

As we sat and chatted, Stevie came over with our meals and as I sat and ate mine I was getting a bit nervous as I knew this was the night that I would properly ask Karen to marry me.

"What's wrong Jonny, you look like you're not enjoying that?"

Again, Karen could read me like a book, every mouthful was like swallowing a brick.

"I am Karen, it's lovely," I replied, trying to wait for the right moment and here it was; as I looked over Karen's shoulder, Stevie had organised a local tribute act to come in and sing so I stopped eating and stood up.

Karen looked up at me, "Jonny, what's wrong?"

"Nothing Karen," I replied. As I walked round to the side of the table I reached into my pocket and got down on one knee.

"Jonny, what are you doing?" Karen said with her face going a bit red.

"Karen, would you do me the honour of marrying me?" I said as held out the open box containing the most beautiful ring, that I had got with the help of Paula I may add.

The place was silent and it felt like an eternity waiting on Karen to answer and then as I looked into her eyes she smiled and replied, "Yes Jonny, I will." She threw her arms round me and kissed me as the whole bar clapped and cheered.

As we sat back in our seats the guy started singing,

it was perfect, really romantic. As we sat and finished our meal, I could enjoy it now, I had a couple more beers before we left for home and as we walked the short journey up the road Karen asked when we were to set the date. I replied, "I know it doesn't give us much time but I was hoping we could get married when your mum and dad is over, what do you think?"

"Jesus Jonny, you don't mess about, it really doesn't give us much time."

"We will be fine, you just worry about a dress, I will organise everything else. We don't need a venue and we know the food will be good."

"What about a church Jonny?"

"I was thinking we could get married right on the beach, it's my most favourite place in the world just looking right over the ocean, it would be perfect."

"That sounds perfect Jonny, oh my god, it's all happening too quickly."

"Life is too short Karen, you have to sometimes just do it and not worry too much, it will be fine, I will do the worrying, you just get your dress."

Karen held my hand that little bit tighter as we walked up the path of our house and gave me a kiss as I put the key in the door. She said, "I love you Jonny Andrews."

"I love you too, the future Mrs Andrews."

We went to bed that night so happy.

Over the next couple of weeks, I had got everything booked and ready for our big day; the invites were sent out and we had decided that we would get married on Wednesday 16th August at 11am in the morning so it wouldn't be too hot. We had 20 people going including Billy and his wife May, I was really looking forward to catching up with him and he also excepted to be my best man.

Karen had got her dress, Paula had taken her to a place in Torrevieja and she was getting so excited as it got closer to our big day.

A few days before our wedding, Karen's mum and dad arrived along with Karen's sister and a few other family members. They had booked into the Presidenti Hotel which was just around the corner from our bar and I think we were both getting really nervous. When Billy and his Mrs arrived the day before the wedding, I was really glad to see him and I think he was really surprised when I brought him to my bar and showed him round. As we walked through the front door he said to me, "You're a long way from the Shankill Road now Jonny, you have done well for yourself son, your bar really is something."

"Thanks Billy, that means a lot, would you like a pint?"

"Jonny, you really do ask the stupidest of questions; of course I will take a pint."

I looked over at Dylan who was behind the bar, "Dylan, can I have two beers please?"

"Yes Jonny, no problem."

As Dylan started pouring the first pint, Billy spoke up, "You may make that four pints Jonny." I looked round and there standing with Billy was Hammy and Brian, I was gob smacked.

"What are you doing here?" I asked in total shock.

"Nice to see you too Jonny boy."

"I don't mean that, I just can't believe you are both here."

"Wouldn't miss it for the world, when Billy told us you were getting married we had to be here and send you off right, so I hope you have nothing planned for the rest of the day mate as we are taking you out on the town."

"Yeah sure but I need to ring Karen first, give me 10 minutes and I will be ready to go."

"Don't worry Jonny, we will look after you," Billy said. Looking at that cheeky smile on his face, I knew I wouldn't be fine but I was looking forward to a day out with them.

I rang Karen and explained to her, she had booked into the Presidenti for the night anyway as it would be easier the next morning and I had planned to stay in Paula's flat as she was staying with Karen to help her get ready. Those plans were out the window now though as god knows where I would end up with these headers.

CHAPTER 7

A Quick Change

A few drinks in the bar and a bite to eat and we were off, it was now 4pm and our first stop was Tiki Beach bar, as per usual it was packed and the atmosphere was electric. I knew the guys that were playing and when they heard I was getting married the next day they tortured the life out of me, they even stuck a learner sign to my back so it wasn't long before I got the attention of most people in the bar and the drinks were flying. We only stayed about an hour and Billy said to me, "Right Jonny boy, let's move on, we have a lot to see and do."

"You're right Billy, this young lad has a lot to learn about getting married and a lot to learn about being the stag," Hammy said and I didn't like the smirk on his face, to be honest, they all looked like they were up to something,

"What do you mean Hammy?" I asked.

"Never you mind Jonny, you're not allowed to ask

questions, let's move on lads, to the next bar."

And at that we walked up towards the strip, as we wandered up the street the warm sun was beating down on us, it was really hot and in turn we all took our t-shirts off. I looked round at the other three, Hammy was like a bean pole, there wasn't a piece of fat on him, Brian on the other hand was smaller and had a beer belly and a hairy chest. Nothing annoyed him, he was really easy going and enjoyed a good laugh, he still thought he was god's gift to the women, I swear you couldn't cut him with a hatchet. Then there was Billy who never changed, he still looked the same as the first day I started working in Heather Street, his dark hair was always in a side shade, he was always immaculately dressed and had a way with him like nobody I had ever met. I only ever saw him lose the rag once and to be honest, I would never mess with him, he had something about him that I just couldn't work out, but over the years I had really got close to him and really respected his opinion and looked up to him.

As we walked across the junction, we looked like something out of a line up from *Crime Watch*. Billy turned round to me and said, "Right Jonny boy, it's time to up the game."

He ushered me into the first bar on the strip and straight away we were on shots, they were rank but after a few we were all going well. Some guy was on singing and the banter was flying, we got a table outside and sat in the sun.

"So Jonny, it's your big day tomorrow?" Brian asked.

"Aye Brian, I am a bit nervous."

"Why would you be nervous? Sure you're living with Karen."

"I know Brian but I haven't written a speech, I was just going to wing it but the more I think about it I should have written something down."

"Fir Christ sake Jonny, worry about that tomorrow, you're out tonight to have fun and fun we are going to have. What time is it now Hammy?" Billy asked.

"5.30 Billy, we have loads of time yet."

"Loads of time for what Billy?"

"Never you mind Jonny, another drink son?"

I was puzzled at what was going on so I just went with the flow, "Aye Billy, get me a bottle of beer this time, the pints are too hard to drink."

"You're a big girl Jonny," Hammy said.

"Get some more vodka shots Billy."

"Don't get me any Billy, I won't make the night if we keep going like this," I said.

Billy went to the bar and brought down yet another tray of drinks, I was really struggling but knew there was no way I could let the side down so every chance I got I drunk a sneaky red bull which seem to do the trick and kept me right.

Bar after bar we visited and by 9 o'clock we were lit to the balls, even Hammy was staggering a bit which surprised me because he never looked drunk. We called into the Red Lion and sat at one of the tables, to be honest I fell into my chair and nearly tipped it over, it was only for Billy putting his hand at my back that I didn't end up on my arse in the middle of the floor so I was glad to be sitting at the table and not in a heap.

More and more drinks and by 10 o'clock when the show started we were blind drunk and it was 'Sticky Vicky' on and she did the usual show for the usual punters. When she finished, the house lights came on and the DJ called out my name, I looked round at Billy and the boys who were laughing. Again, the DJ called my name and this time Billy ushered me to a single chair in the middle of the room and sat me down.

The DJ handed a mic to Billy, "Good evening everybody," Billy said.

"This is Jonny who is getting married tomorrow," which got a huge cheer from everyone, I could feel my face going red.

"You are all in for a treat as we intend to give him a good send-off," again the bar cheered and Billy looked over at the DJ who started playing some music, the house lights went down and as I sat there a bit worried what was going to happen Billy whispered into my ear, "Have fun Jonny."

I just looked at him as he walked back over to the table where Hammy and Brian were. I noticed over their shoulders that two good looking girls dressed in police uniforms were walking towards me and I knew then what was coming, I looked at the lads who just gave me the thumbs up and laughed.

Both girls came over to me and started dancing, one of them was behind me and her hands were all over me and I mean all over me. She took my t-shirt off and got me to stand up, the other girl in-front of me unbuttoned my jeans and pulled them down. She got me to sit back down again, as she knelt down she started removing my shoes then my socks then my jeans. She then started to get me to undress her and as I slowly unbuttoned her top, the crowd was going nuts I swear I heard Brian shout, "Get them off."

Both of these girls were some shape, pure belters, all the bumps in the right places; it was when I had them both undressed to their underwear they got me to stop which got a sigh from the crowd. As the music stopped I thought that was it over but no, it had only begun.

The girl that was in-front of me started straddling me and at that stage she was dry humping me, she grabbed my head and pulled it into her boobs and again rubbed herself up and down me. She was moaning and groaning and I honestly think at one stage she was really getting off on me, the crowd was going mad, cheering and whistling. She stood up and took a step back, as I looked at her she licked her lips and then put her finger in her mouth and walked back over to me and placed her finger in my mouth. The sad thing was I wasn't even tied up, I could have got up at any stage and stopped it but to be honest it was bloody brilliant, how could you not enjoy it? Two good looking blondes give you a lap dance like the way they were? She then stepped back again and looked over my shoulder at her mate who then put a belt round my neck and got me to get on all fours like a dog which I didn't even put up a struggle against. Her mate got on my back and she walked me round the bar a couple of times looking like a bloody header, but it was good fun. As we got to the middle of the floor again, she got off and I went to stand up but wasn't allowed, I was just told to stay where I was as another song came on and then it happened…

Out came the whip again which brought back bad memories, I wasn't looking forward to this but it is what it is, and *crack* across my back. It sobered me up in a second, a few more whips and my back was on fire, even the crowd were wincing as I got a couple more. I was then stood up as one of the girls got down on her knees and tried to remove my boxer shorts, I knew what was coming and was having none of it. I looked at Billy who knew by my face that this wasn't going to happen, he immediately came over and got the girl to stand up, he spoke into her ear and at the disappointment of the crowd they finished off the song by rubbing themselves up and down me. When they finished the crowd yelled for more but to my relief it was over and I was able to get dressed, Billy went on the mic again.

"I hope you all enjoyed that as much as I did and I would like to invite you all for a complementary drink at Buffaloes bar tomorrow night to help young Jonny here celebrate his marriage."

At that a big cheer went up but I'm sure Billy could see my face, I wasn't happy to say the least at the thought of all these headers turn up to my bar tomorrow night and especially giving drink away but it was too late now and I just had to roll with it and hope none of them turned up.

As I got dressed again and walked back to the table, punter after punter wished me all the best for the next day and gave me a pat on the back. The first couple weren't too bad but then my back started stinging and as another big lad hit me on the back I was in a bit of pain and I winced a bit and the lads started laughing, they thought it was hilarious to say the least.

One of the bar staff came down and set us up a free drink and handed me two tablets, he said, "Take these mate, they will help with the pain."

I looked at him and asked, "What are they?"

"Just pain killers mate," he winked at Billy as he said that and I should have realised then that they weren't pain killers but I took them anyway and washed them down with a pint.

As we moved on to the next bar we were all having a laugh about the strippers and the lap dance that I got. I asked Billy, "Where the hell did you find them mate?"

"A mate back home got me their number and he told me we wouldn't be disappointed, and he was right, we all loved it, you were hilarious Jonny."

"Aye I know but you weren't on the receiving end Billy, it wasn't too funny where I was looking from, my back is still bloody sore, them tablets aren't working at all."

"They must take a while come on, we will call in here for one," Billy pointed to the next bar and as we walked into the place I felt a bit funny.

I turned to Hammy and said, "Fuck Hammy, I don't feel right."

"What do you mean Jonny, are you going to be sick?"

"No I don't think so," just as I was going to tell him how I felt I could feel my dick going hard.

"Fuck, fuck, fuck," I said.

"What's wrong Jonny?" Brian asked as the three of them started laughing.

"As if you three fuckers don't know, you have set me up again, they were fucking Viagra weren't they?"

The three of them couldn't speak for laughing.

"How long does this last?" I asked as I was now fully erect and couldn't hide the bloody thing. I was standing there pointing at everyone with a bloody hard on, they laughed even more when they all noticed my bulge in my jeans.

In fact, everyone in the bar started noticing it and this girl said as she walked past, "Alright big boy, I take it you're glad to see me."

I was totally scundered, my face was beaming and Billy and the lads were now laughing that hard tears were running down their cheeks.

"For fuck sake Billy, what am I going to do with this thing?"

Through the laughing Billy replied, "I don't know Jonny but keep it away from me," and he continued laughing.

I noticed a free table and quickly sat down at it to hide my now throbbing penis, the boys joined me and started calming down. Hammy went and got the drinks in and I was now getting the attention of a few other girls that were pointing over and laughing.

"This is a night I'm going to remember for a long

time Billy."

"You really will Jonny."

Hammy came down with the drinks and handed me a bit of paper.

"Here Jonny, I was asked to give you this."

As I opened it up I asked, "What is it Hammy?"

"A telephone number mate."

"What, from who?"

"That good looker standing at the bar," as he turned and pointed I looked up from the piece of paper. The bar was quite full so I didn't know who he was pointing at. "Who Hammy?" I asked again as I tried to work out whose number it was.

"The blonde Jonny," he replied and laughed.

As I looked up at the bar the only blonde that was there was the huge big lad that had squeezed himself into a way too tight white t-shirt and as I caught his eye he blew me a kiss and waved.

"For fuck sake, could this night get any worse?"

The lads started laughing again.

"We aren't staying here, if that big lad gets the hold of me I'm done for, so drink up lads, we are leaving."

"Wise up Jonny, you're safe with us."

"It's you lot I'm worried about, come on, this bar's crap, we will move up the road a bit."

We lashed our drinks into us and as we were about to leave, I needed a piss so I said to the lads to hold fire as I went into the toilets.

As I stood there at one of the urinals I unbuttoned my jeans and who bloody walked in but the guy in the white t-shirt. I couldn't even look at him and as I tried in vain to have a piss it bloody was going everywhere, I even think I splashed the big lad a bit too and he wasn't happy. He said to me, "My goodness, you are a big lad," as he looked down at my dick.

I replied, "You have no idea mate, the guys I'm with thought it was funny to give me two Viagra and I'm stuck with this thing."

"Seems a shame to waste it, my hotel is just round the corner."

'What the fuck?' I thought.

"You're ok mate, I don't bat on your team if you know what I mean."

"I do and she is a lucky girl tonight alright."

He winked at me and turned and washed his hands, as I was still struggling to have a piss he said, "Have a good night good looking."

I didn't even answer him, I was trying to tuck my dick back into my jeans and try and make it not so obvious looking. I then washed my hands and left.

The lads were waiting outside and as I looked at my watch it was now 12.50, Billy said to me, "Come on Jonny, we have a couple more bars to get to."

"Billy I'm going to call it a night, I have a big day tomorrow."

"No chance Jonny lad, you're not going home until we have to carry you," Hammy said as he put his arm round my neck and started walking me up the street. There was no chance I was getting an early night so it was into the rock club where The Beatles tribute was about to come on.

The place was bunged so it was standing room only at the bar where Billy had set up a round of shots and it was down the hatch they went. More and more drink was put in front of me, I think I lasted about another hour or so but by then I was well gone and I didn't remember another thing after that.

As I opened my eyes the sun was really bright, I was lying on a sunbed on the beach; as I sat up my head was spinning and pounding like a jack hammer, I leant over and threw up, I was an absolute mess. I looked at my watch and it was 6.45am. "Thank Christ," I said as I stood up and looked around, the beach was empty apart from a few birds scavenging for scraps and it was so quiet, only the sound of the waves crashing against the rocks. My head started spinning again and I threw up, I had to sit back down on the sunbed again, I was in a state. My stomach was churning and I retched and retched as I had nothing left in my belly to be sick with.

I sat for a while and then realised my phone was missing and my wallet, shit, I must have been robbed and where was Billy and the lads? I started getting really worried, I looked at my watch, 7.10am and I realised that I didn't recognise this part of the beach. I stood up again, I couldn't even see the famous rock that sat in the middle of Benidorm bay, where the hell was I? I started staggering up the beach and onto the promenade, as I walked a guy was picking litter up, I stopped him.

"Excuse me senor but where am I?"

"No English," the guy shook his head and just held his arms out.

I tried again, "What town is this?"

He pointed to a sign above my head, it read Torrevieja Playa, my heart sunk, I knew then where I was and I looked at my watch: 7.30am. I was a good hour's drive from Benidorm but that's if I was driving, what the hell was I going to do? How was I getting back to Karen? We were due to get married at 11am. I looked down at myself and the state of me, I was a mess, I needed to get back and get changed. I searched my pockets again in a real panic, I emptied them onto a bench, I had about 10 euro in change and a piece of paper. I unfolded it and as I was about to read it the guy touched me on the shoulder, "Senor, adios mi amigo."

I thanked him and he carried on lifting litter from the promenade, I got back to reading the note, it read, *'Just make it to Buffaloes by 10 and you will be fine, lots of love Billy.'*

"Fuckers," I said aloud, I hadn't been robbed, them gits had left me here and I bet you they are still laughing.

I walked up through the streets trying to find the bus station and the longer time went by the more in a panic I got. As I was about to give up I heard a car horn, I stopped and looked around and it was a big black Jeep, the windows where tinted so I couldn't see who was driving. I looked around to see if it was me he was tooting at and this time I heard the door open. "Jonny, Jonny Andrews?"

I looked at him, "Yes it is." It hit me, it was the guy

I had pulled from the car, I couldn't believe my eyes.

"What are you doing here Jonny?"

"It's a long story, I was on my stag night and ended up here, I really need to get back to Benidorm, I am getting married at 11."

"Then jump in, I will take you."

"Super." I got into his motor and off we went.

It was a beautiful big Jeep, lovely leather seats and the dash board lit up like the cockpit of a plane, it was gorgeous. I turned and said, "This is some motor, what is it?"

"It's an Audi, do you like it Jonny?"

"I do mate, it's some motor."

As we drove up the motorway we chatted some more, I asked, "I never caught your name?"

"I know Jonny, that day of the accident was a blur, we never got introduced properly. I'm Roy Greer and to be honest I owe you more than a lift, if it wasn't for you I wouldn't be here today."

"I didn't do anything nobody else wouldn't have done."

"No Jonny, you did and I will never forget it."

We drove on further, I was feeling rough again and couldn't wait to get back to Buffaloes and get a shower.

"So Jonny, what are the plans for today?"

"Try and not throw up is going to be the main plan, I'm dying a death here, but I'll have to get back and get ready, as I told you I'm getting married at 11 o'clock."

I looked at my watch as I said that and it was now 9.30 and I was starting to get nervous, we were about 10 minutes away and I was in a bit of a panic.

"You will be fine Jonny, you have loads of time, a shower and a shave and you will feel better, have you got everything organised?"

"Yeah I think so, we are getting married on the beach and then just going back to the bar for a meal and then a group is coming on, so it should be a good day."

"Who have you got singing?"

"They are called the Mavericks, they are pretty good."

"Aye, I used to have them on my books a few years back."

"What do you mean on your books?"

"I look after most of the tribute acts that do the circuit."

"That sounds like a really interesting job."

"It is Jonny, your future wife, who does she like?"

"Jesus, I don't know, why?"

"Might be able to get them to do a set tonight for you."

I took a minute and thought who Karen would love to hear, and then it hit me.

"She loves Prince."

"Brilliant, the tribute act I have does a really good set as Prince, hold on, I will give him a ring."

At that Roy touched a screen on the dash board and a dial tone came through the radio speakers, he flicked down a list and then touched the name 'Prince' and it started to dial the number. I was flabbergasted, *holy shit this car is something else,* a guy answered, "Hi Roy, what's up?"

"I'm looking for a favour, can you do a set tonight for me?"

"What time and where?"

"It's a bar called Buffaloes in Benidorm, and could you go on at 10 o'clock?"

"Anything for you Roy, what's the occasion?"

"It is a good friend of mine, he is getting married today and it would be a real treat as his Mrs is a big fan. It would be a massive surprise for her to have you sing on their wedding day."

"That's fine Roy, I will be there for 9.30 to get set up."

"Thanks Jim, I will see you later."

At that Roy touched another button on the screen and the call was finished, then the music came back on again. I was speechless, Roy turned to me and said, "That's that sorted Jonny, all that's left is to get you cleaned up and ready for your big day."

"Thanks Roy, Karen will be over the moon, it will really make her day."

"I told you Jonny, I am in your debt for a long time and anything you need I will make myself available."

"That means a lot Roy, thanks."

Roy pulled his car outside my bar, I turned to him and said, "Would you and your better half like to come for dinner later and join us after the wedding?"

"I wouldn't miss it for the world Jonny, what time?"

"Around 3 would be fine."

Roy put his hand out and I shook it as Roy said, "I will see you later then Jonny, and good luck with the wedding."

"Thanks Roy, I will see you later for a beer."

I got out of Roy's car and closed the door, as it drove away I stood and admired it. I said to myself, *'Someday I am going to treat Karen and me to a motor like that.'*

I turned and walked into the bar and there and behold was Billy and the lads sitting round a table having a pint. As they turned to look at me they cheered and all stood up, they were already changed and to be fair they all looked really well, but by the look on my face the cheers didn't last long. I walked over and said, "Fuck sake lads, what happened last night?"

They just laughed and Billy said, "It was a good night Jonny, we knew you would make it back." Billy looked at his watch and said, "Not before time too, you better get your skates on, it's 10 o'clock."

"Shit," I said as I looked at my own watch, I turned to walk out and go to Paula's flat to get changed but Hammy handed me a bottle of beer and a bacon bap.

"Get this down you Jonny, it will sort you out."

I took the bacon bap and bottle of beer off him, my stomach churned as the smell of the smoky bacon filled my nose and I started retching. I set the beer and bap on the table and quickly dashed to the toilets where I boked my ring up. As I knelt on my knees with my arms around the toilet bowl, I retched and couldn't be sick anymore; tears streamed down my cheeks as I stood up and I coughed a couple of times and spat the rest of the sick that was stuck in my throat down the toilet. I lifted some toilet roll and blew my nose and tried to get myself together, I flushed the chain and as I walked over to the basins I was dizzy and the thought of letting Karen down on our wedding day was enough to make me get myself together. I turned the cold water tap on and cupped my hands under it, they filled with ice cold water, I bent down and threw the water round my face, it sent shivers down my spine but it felt good. I did it again and again until I started feeling a bit better, so I dried my face with the paper towels and walked back out to the bar. Billy was standing, he walked over, "Jonny go up and get a shower and get your suit on, I will get you some breakfast ready and a coffee." Billy put his arm round me and ushered me to the door, he walked me the short distance to Paula's flat and then said, "It's a quick turnaround son, you only have about half an hour before we need to leave."

"No worries Billy, I will be as quick as I can."

I put the key in the lock and opened Paula's flat door and walked upstairs and straight into the bathroom where I got undressed and got into the shower. I got washed and dried as quickly as I could, then I had a quick shave and got my smellies on. I got dressed in my lovely new grey suit, put a bit of gel in my hair and I didn't feel too bad. I put my shoes on and I was ready for the off.

I went back into the bar where Billy and the lads had a fry up set up for me and a cup of coffee. I went and sat with them, Brian turned to me, "You look a lot better now Jonny, get that down you and you will be ready for anything."

I choked the fry up down and as I finished my coffee Hammy said, "Right lads, let's get this show on the road."

We all got up and headed for the door, as I caught my breath walking out of the bar I paused for a moment. "Well here goes Jonny," Hammy said as Billy opened the door and there parked right outside the bar was the biggest limo I had ever seen.

As I walked over to the motor Billy looked at me, "Well Jonny, your chariot awaits."

I looked at my watch: 10.40. "Holly shit Billy, we need to go."

"Not just yet Jonny, we need a photo." Some girl was standing with a camera and we all stood beside the car and got a photo; the driver came walking over and opened the door, we all got in, even the girl with the camera and she took a couple of photos as we made the short trip round to Levante beach.

CHAPTER 8

I Do

As the car pulled up right on the promenade we got out of the limo one by one, we all stood and admired what I had set up for our wedding; there was red carpet the length of the walkway which led down right to the water's edge where I had 20 seats all set up under a marquee and at the front was the local magistrate waiting to marry us. I turned to Billy, "Well mate, what do you think?"

"It's perfect Jonny, it's just bloody perfect."

We posed for some more photos before making the short walk down to the water's edge. I shook the magistrates hand and thanked him for doing this on such short notice, just then a few taxis started arriving and our friends had arrived - not before time as it wasn't too long after that when the limo arrived again and Karen's mum, dad, sister and Paula got out, closely followed by Karen. She was stunning, she was dressed in the most beautiful wedding dress and her hair and makeup was immaculate, I really was a lucky man to have such a beautiful girl about to marry me. I stood there proud as punch as Karen was getting a few photos taken, Karen's mum Linda and her sister Kellie came walking down the red carpet and took their seats at the front which were now the only seats left as everyone that we had invited had arrived and were patiently waiting for it to start. As I stood there with Billy at my side I was slightly nervous and a bead of sweat ran down my forehead and down my cheek, I wiped it away with the back of my hand and Billy turned to me and said, "Jonny, relax, try and enjoy the day, it will be over before you know it."

"I will Billy, it's getting really warm, I'm sweating."

"I know son, these suits don't help but I'm sure we will be fine a wee pint later that will taste better once we get this bit out of the way."

At that I spotted Karen starting to walk down the aisle holding her dad's arm, she was smiling when I caught her eye and she smiled that little bit more; as she came walking towards me my heart was thumping, when her dad left her by my side she took my hand, I leant in and kissed her on the cheek and said, "You look beautiful, I love you."

"I love you too," she replied.

As we stood there and exchanged vows it was just how I imagined it, looking out over the sea the magistrate was speaking about marriage and what it meant, my thoughts wondered and I was thinking about how my mum would have loved it and as I glanced slightly upwards I wondered if she was looking down.

Karen squeezed my hand, as I looked at her a tear ran down my cheek, I quickly wiped it away as Karen said softly, "Are you ok Jonny?"

I smiled as I replied, "Yeah Karen, I am."

I squeezed her hand back and the magistrate said, "And who has the rings?"

I looked round at Billy who had his arm out stretched and handed me the two rings. "Thanks Billy," I said as I set the rings on the open book the magistrate was holding.

We exchanged the rest of our vows and then we each in turn placed the rings on each other's finger and as we kissed everyone stood up and clapped, I even heard Hammy shout, "Get a room," which got a laugh.

We then signed the register and we were married.

I had organised champagne for everyone and as we all stood under the marquee out of the warm sun we chatted with everyone there.

Alan came over to me and said, "Jonny, can I have a word?" I was sort of taken back a bit, with Karen's dads tone it sounded serious.

"Yes Alan," I told him.

Alan put his arm round my shoulder, we walked to the water's edge and he said to me, "Jonny, I have known you for a while now and I know Karen loves you and I know you love her as well but I need to know something."

"What is it Alan?"

"I need to know my Karen is safe here in Spain, I know you were mixed up in some serious things back in Belfast."

"Alan, I will stop you there, that life was forced on me and we don't live in Belfast and I assure you I never want to return to that life. My life is with Karen and our kids, when they are born."

"That's all I wanted to hear son, welcome to the family." Alan threw his arms round me and hugged me, I looked over his shoulder as I hugged him back and I spotted Karen watching over, she smiled and I smiled back.

We got a few more photos taken and I asked everyone to start to make their way up to Buffaloes where we would have a few drinks and get the speeches out of the way.

We got back into the limo where we went for some more photos, I think I got to the stage where my smile was painted on and I think Karen was the same. When we got back to the bar we got a cheer as we walked through the front doors, Peter had the place set up really nice, all the tables had lovely table cloths on and a fish bowl on its centre with twinkly lights, they all had nice wine glasses and a couple of bottles of wine on each table, all the chairs had covers on them with matching bows around them - it made the place look really fancy. The group we had booked were already playing and the party was in full flow.

Billy handed me a pint, "Alright Jonny lad, get that down you."

He leant over and kissed Karen on the cheek, "Congratulations love, you have got yourself a good one here."

As he put his arm round my neck Karen said, "I

think you will find Billy that Jonny is the lucky one," she laughed, her laugh was infectious and we all stood laughing. I took a gulp of my pint and it was so refreshing on such a hot day, the air con in the bar was on full blast but it was still really warm, suppose wearing a suit didn't help matters. I took another few gulps of my pint, my hangover was the furthest thing from my mind now. We stood chatting for a while but the moment had arrived that I had been dreading: the speeches.

As we all took our places at the tables, I noticed Roy was sitting near the back with his wife sitting beside him, I waved over and he waved back. *.So here goes,* I heard the band stop playing and I was handed a mic, I had many a tortured night trying to write down what to say and had myself worried sick but it wasn't me who had to speak first so I introduced Karen's dad Alan and handed him the mic. He said some really nice things about how proud he was of both of us and wished us both all the happiness and wealth in the world, he got a round of applause and then it was me...

"Thank you Alan for your kind words, it really means a lot to us both." I turned to Karen, "Karen, you are everything to me, life with you is a dream and sometimes I have to pinch myself just make sure I am not sleeping."

I had to take a breath and felt really nervous talking in front of everyone.

"You are absolutely stunning, and so are both your bridesmaids, your dress is beautiful and I have to thank you for saying yes to be my wife." I got a cheer from the crowd which made my face go a bit red, you would think I was about 18 again, but I really didn't enjoy speaking in front of everyone.

"I would like to thank Billy for being my best man and for the lads who made my stag night what it was - ending up 50 miles away with a stinker of a hangover. I would also like to thank Roy for the much needed lift home and for saving the day." I nodded over at Roy and then I asked everyone to be up standing and toast the bride and her bridesmaids, I then sat down with a massive sigh of relief as it was Billy's turn.

He really ripped into me and had the crowd in stitches but it was when he started talking about my life back in Belfast and losing my mum, dad and nanny followed by him telling me how he felt about me and how I was like the son he never had that even had a tear run down my cheek. It was a really poignant moment when he turned to me and told me he was really proud of me and would always be by my side when I needed him. I choked back my tears and stood up and hugged him, we gripped each other really tightly and everyone stood up and clapped, it was really nice to have that moment and then I think it got to the point where we both needed a pint. We sat down and I swear I had two big gulps of my pint and it was finished.

Billy opened the floor up to see if anyone wanted to say anything and I was glad that nobody did, I was an emotional wreck and Karen knew it. As she held my hand under the table and squeezed it really tightly she looked at me, "That was nice of Billy, Jonny?"

"Yeah Karen, it was, I love you, do you know that?"

"I do Jonny and I love you too."

It was a relief that all the speeches were over and it was time for Peter and the staff to serve the meal, and what a meal it was. We had pate on melba toast to start, Karen had organised the menu and I had no idea what we were getting or what pate was but it was beautiful, really tasty, but it really didn't do much for my now rumbling stomach. I was starving and when the next course came out my eyes lit up, my favourite: steak with champ and all the trimmings and when I say all the trimmings, the way Peter cooked the vegetables was superb, carrots and parsnips all cut to finger length and roasted in sugar, they melted in your mouth. As per usual the steaks were really good and smothered in pepper sauce, it really did hit the spot, I swear I don't think I said a word for a good ten minutes I was enjoying my dinner that much.

We had a bit of a break before our desert came, it gave Karen and I a chance to go and speak with our friends and family, well that was Karen's thing as for me it was dragged to the bar with the lads. After a couple of rounds of shots and a pint, the day was getting more like a party now, the banter was flying, even Karen's dad Alan got in on the craic.

Peter came out of the kitchen and told me desert was ready to be served so we all took our seats and got tucked into a huge whack of Pavlova covered in fresh cream and strawberries with strawberry sauce, it just finished the meal perfectly.

After we had all finished, the staff that Peter had brought in cleared the tables in a flash and as we all sort of gathered at the bar, a few of the tables were taken out to make room for the dance floor and the night was now in full flow.

A few more people started coming in and at one point I had to serve behind the bar we were that busy, but I got the shepherd's hook from Karen and ushered onto the dance floor. Here we had the first slow dance and as we danced for that few minutes of the song, everything was perfect, life couldn't get any better, as the song finished we kissed.

Roy nobbled me at the bar.

"Jonny, Prince will be here in about half an hour, can I introduce him when he comes in? What would you like him to play first?"

"Jesus Roy, I wouldn't have a clue, just get him to play his usual."

"That's fine Jonny, you won't be disappointed."

I looked at my watch and it was now 9.30, I thought to myself, *'Where the hell has this day went?'*

I looked over at Karen who was up dancing with her sister, Paula and her mum, she looked really happy. I felt a hand on my shoulder, I looked round and it was Billy, "A pint Jonny?"

"Oh yes Billy, I could murder one."

As we stood at the bar Billy said to me ,"Jonny, you have done really well for yourself over here, have you ever thought about coming home?"

"I have Billy but I don't think I ever will, my life is here in Spain and when the babies are born there is no way I would move back to the Shankill, there is too much to risk. I could never trust Sam, I would always be looking over my shoulder."

"You're probably right Jonny, the only thing that has changed on the road is that Sam is running things from inside the jail, I would love to get away from it all as well, it's not enjoyable anymore working in the club."

I don't know if it was the drink talking or what Billy had said in his speech but I had a brain wave and I then said to Billy, "Then why don't you move out here Billy? Why don't come and run Buffaloes? It would take a lot of the pressure off me."

"Seriously Jonny, are you sure you know what you are asking?"

"Billy, I would love for you to come and work here and I think you would love it as well."

"Jesus Jonny, I wasn't expecting that, I would have to sell up and I mean sell everything and then there is the wife, I would have to talk her into it…"

"Well Billy, the offer is there."

Billy threw his arms around me and as we stood there I could see Karen coming over. She walked up to us and I could read her lips as she mouthed the words, "Is everything ok?"

"Karen, I have asked Billy to come and work for us and I think if his wife agrees he is going to move out."

"Billy, that would be fantastic."

I wasn't sure how Karen would react but I think she knew what I thought of Billy and what Billy thought of me.

"Karen love I'm not sure if my wife would up sticks and move, it's a lot to ask but you never know, when I get back home I will ask her and see if she is up for a new life in the sun."

"Give her a ring now Billy," I said.

"No Jonny, I would have to see her face to face, it is too big of a decision, but I will do my best. I can see why you both love it out here, it really is a lovely life."

Karen squeezed my hand, "I will leave you boys to have a beer, I need the toilet." She kissed me on the cheek .

"No worries love," I replied. Karen couldn't have timed going to the toilet better, as when she turned to leave Roy came over with his act for the night.

"Hi Jonny, this is Jim I was telling you about."

"Hi Jim, thanks for doing this, my wife is going to love you."

There was something not right and I couldn't work it out, he was a small man, about 5ft with longish curly dark hair, he was wearing the tightest trousers I had ever seen and a shirt opened up to his waist. He really was a strange looking bloke but I suppose if Roy recommended him he must be good.

Jim replied, "No worries Jonny, Roy has looked after me for years so it's not a problem, could I get a drink before I get changed?"

"Yeah, what would you like?"

"Just Vodka."

"What would you like as a mixer?"

"Nothing, just ice."

I looked at Roy and he just laughed as he slapped Jim on the shoulder, he said, "You never surprise me Jim."

In the 15 minutes that we stood there Jim knocked five vodkas into him, I thought Billy and the lads could drink but this was a different level.

He then went and got changed, I turned to Roy and said, "Where did you find him? He is strange looking, Roy."

Roy just laughed, "I know he doesn't look like much but wait and see him when he comes out, you will love him Jonny."

"I don't know Roy, by the time he comes out he will be plastered after knocking them vodkas into him so quick."

"Stop panicking Jonny, he puts on a good show."

Roy went up to the group and asked them to finish the next song and take a break for an hour, he told them that his act was coming on.

I went down and sat beside Karen, I was a bit drunk but having a good night, I wanted to see her reaction when Prince came on.

"Hi love, are you having a good night?"

"I am Jonny, but I am getting a bit tired, it won't be long before I'm off to bed."

I looked at my watch, it was now 10 o'clock and Roy came up to the mic, "Hello everyone, I hope you are all having a good night." At that everyone cheered. "I would like to introduce our main act for the night." He leant over and pressed play on the mixer box that Jim had set up, he flicked another switch and the lights went out just leaving a single light in the middle of the dance floor. As the music started, the back door of the bar opened and all I can say is everyone's jaw hit the floor when Prince, or should I say Princess, came strutting in to the music.

I looked at Karen and she looked at me, we were both in shock; Jim was wearing a full tight fitting dress with the biggest high heels you have ever seen, but he strolled across the floor singing *Kiss* by Prince and he was fantastic. Everyone laughed at first but then got up and started dancing, it was brilliant and really funny as Jim danced around everyone singing.

He put on a fantastic show, we both really loved it, the only time he stopped singing was in-between a couple of songs when he tortured the life out of everyone there. Billy got a real ripping and I was surprised he didn't even have a comeback, he just took it and laughed, it really was a brilliant night but it had to come to an end and by 12 o'clock we wrapped it up and Karen and I got a taxi home and went straight to bed as we were both shattered.

The next few days we said our goodbyes to everyone as they had to go back home and life went back to normal.

Billy had talked his wife into moving to Spain and was in the process of selling his house and getting plans put in place to come and work in Buffaloes. Karen only had a couple of months left before the babies were due and we got things ready, decorating their room and buying some more furniture and baby things, everything was getting exciting as the weeks ticked by.

CHAPTER 9

A Fortnight Early

Billy and his wife Mary had made the decision that they were to move out to Spain, but it wouldn't be until the following year as Mary was studying to be a nurse and had 6 months to complete which I think suited Billy as he wanted to get the house sold and tie up loose ends. He made a few trips over in the next few weeks looking for a house to buy and he had decided on one near ours, in fact only two streets away. I think Billy couldn't wait but he knew the timing had to be right and on the last time he was over finalising the house he said that he wouldn't be back over until everything back home was sorted and he was really looking forward to a new start.

As for me and Karen we only had 2 weeks left before our babies were due and every day was like a week. I felt really sorry for Karen, she was really struggling god love her, she was the size of a house and to make it worse she had a pregnancy itch which was driving her insane. The weather was roasting, even in November it was still 30 degrees, so she spent most of her time in the house with the air-conditioning on just to stay cool.

One night after work I got home around 8pm, I walked into the house, Karen was sitting watching TV, she had a worried look on her face.

"What's wrong Karen?"

"Jonny, I have been getting these pains all day, I think the babies are coming."

I went into a full panic, "Shit, we will have to get to the hospital." I ran around the house like a head case getting Karen's bag and a few other bits and pieces.

"Jonny, for Christ sake, calm down, I'm ok."

"No you're not, the babies are coming, we have to get to the hospital." The sweat was running out of me. "Come on, we've got to go."

"Relax Jonny, the pains have been coming and going all day."

Karen was so calm, I gave her my hand and helped her to her feet and we headed for the car. As I locked the front door I turned to see Karen waddle down the steps and to the parked car, she really was struggling, I ran down the steps and got the door for her and helped her get in. She clenched my hand really tightly as another contraction came. "Karen are you ok?" I asked as the flow of blood was now stopping going to my fingers. She winced in pain and started panting; I clenched my teeth together as my hand started going numb, the pain was getting unbearable, my hand was starting to turn purple. The contraction started easing as Karen's grip eased as well, I got my hand back and opened and closed my fist a couple of times to try to get the blood flow going again.

Karen said, "That was a strong one Jonny."

'No shit,' I thought, my hand was aching. "Was it love?" I said. "Are you ok?"

"Yeah Jonny, I think you were right about going to the hospital."

I closed Karen's door and walked round the back of the car, rubbing my hand I thought to myself, *'Just get to the hospital before she crushes it again.'*

I got into the car and started the drive to the hospital which was normally about 20 minutes away and in that short period of time Karen had another two contractions. I was smart this time, I kept my hands firmly on the steering wheel as Karen panted and moaned while the pain gripped her. We arrived at the hospital and I just parked outside the front doors; I got out and ran round and opened Karen's door, she looked at me and said, "For frigs sake Jonny, will you calm down? I'm ok."

I didn't know what to say as I helped Karen out of the car, I helped her in through the front doors of the maternity ward and we went straight up to reception where we were greeted by an elderly woman, "Hola, can I help you?"

Karen replied, "I think I am in labour."

"You think?" I replied. "She has been getting pains all day."

"Have you got your file with you?" the girl asked.

Karen reached into the side of her bag and passed her file to the girl who opened it and started typing her details into the computer which was in front of her.

"I see you're not due for another 2 weeks but I also see you are expecting twins so you might be going early, we will get you looked at by one of the doctors. Can you take a seat and we will see you as soon as a doctor is free?"

"Thank you," Karen replied as she turned and waddled to a row of seats behind us, I just followed like a lost lamb.

As we sat chatting Karen had another contraction and she grabbed my leg and Jesus, she squeezed the life out of it. I braved it out but it was bloody sore and when the girl called Karen's name to go to room four, it couldn't have came quicker. Karen's contraction eased and I stood up with my now dead leg and helped her to her feet, as Karen waddled over to room four I limped behind her, I'm sure if anyone was watching us they would have said, 'Look at the state of your man, he is walking like he is the one that's pregnant.'

As we entered the room the doctor was waiting, he greeted us and asked Karen to lie down on the bed. I helped Karen get on to the bed and stood holding her hand, praying she never had another contraction. As the doctor finished his examination he said, "Yes Karen, you are in labour, you are about five centimetres dilated so you will be a while yet, we will get you admitted and get you more comfortable."

We both looked at each other, I said to Karen, "This is really happening love."

She held my hand, "Yes Jonny, it is, can you ring my mum and let her know?"

"Yes love, I will once you get booked in."

It didn't take long until we were brought round to a private room, Karen was starting to look really tired, the doctor had asked what pain relief she wanted and Karen only asked for Gas and Air, if it was me I would have taken everything they offered.

I rang Karen's mum and dad to let them know what was happening and they were really excited to hear the news.

It was a really long night but the next morning at nine minutes past ten our babies were born, a beautiful baby boy was first and as the nurse cleaned him up and weighed him our daughter was born and she was gorgeous as well. Poor Karen was exhausted, it really did take it out of her, but when she held both our babies her pain was no more, she was glowing and just smiled and kissed the babies' heads. I had a tear run down my cheek as I stood and watched them, it was just perfect and the feeling of being a daddy was like no other feeling in the world.

I leant in and kissed Karen, "I love you Karen, you have made me the happiest man in the world." I then kissed both the babies on the head. "I love you both as well, your mummy and me will love you both forever and never let anyone hurt you." I kissed them both again and then kissed Karen.

Karen said, "I love you too Jonny."

Karen was wrecked, one of the nurses came over and said, "Can we take the babies and put them in their cots? We need to get you cleaned up Karen."

Karen smiled and said, "Yes, of course you can."

At that both babies were then taken over to where two cots where sitting and they were laid down. The nurse then said to me, "Jonny, could you go for a coffee for 20 minutes while we get Karen sorted?"

"Yeah, no worries," I replied and gave Karen a kiss and told her I would see her in a bit.

As I walked down the corridor I was walking on air, I rang Karen's mum and dad to give them the good news, they told me they had booked flights and were coming out in 3 days' time. As I sat in the coffee shop I rang Billy to tell him our news, he was chuffed to bits for us but he had news of his own which wasn't so good, he told me he was having trouble selling the club as Sam had put a stop to the sale and he didn't know what to do. I told him I would ring him the next day, it worried me that Sam had put pressure on him as I knew what he was capable of.

When I returned to our room to see Karen and the babies Karen was asleep, it really had taken it out of her. The nurses were sitting feeding the babies, they were beautiful, I walked over to admire my babies and as I stood there one of the nurses asked me, "Would you like to feed him?"

My heart skipped a beat but I replied, "Yes, I would love to."

The nurse stood up and asked me to sit on the seat when she placed my son in my arms, I was frightened at first that I would hurt him, he was so small and helpless, but the nurse told me to relax and as I placed the bottle of milk in his mouth he just latched onto the teat. Oh my goodness, he was a hungry boy, the nurse had to tell me to stop feeding him and to wind him, again my heart was in my mouth as I placed my hand just under his chin and gently rubbed his back, a big burp came up and I was so proud of him. "Well done wee man," I said as another burp came up, this time some of his bottle came up with it and ended up on my jeans but I didn't care, this was my son and no matter what he did I was so proud of him. The other nurse was feeding my daughter and she was a good feeder as well, the nurse was a natural at feeding her and she had her fed and winded in a flash and she then changed her nappy and had her back down in her cot and sleeping. I opted out of the nappy change and let the nurse finish him off and get him sorted and into his cot.

I stayed for a while longer just watching my babies and couldn't believe how beautiful they were, they were so small but just perfect.

I went over to Karen and kissed her on the head, I said softly, "I will see you later love, get a good rest."

She sort of answered back, but she fell straight back to sleep again.

As I walked out of the hospital it was another scorcher of a day, I looked at my phone and I had missed a call from Paula so I gave her a ring to let her know that the babies were born. She was in a bit of a panic as it was festival week in Benidorm and the drinks delivery hadn't come, I told her I would get it sorted and to just keep things ticking over until I got there later on.

I made a few phone calls and was told the delivery would be there for 2pm, I also gave Billy a ring, it was worrying me a bit about Sam and his henchmen putting pressure on him.

"Morning mate, how's things going?"

"Jonny, how's Karen and the babies?"

"Just perfect mate, everything is fine, what's happening with you and the club?"

"Don't be worrying about that Jonny, I will get it sorted, just you enjoy your babies, have you any names picked?"

"We have a couple of names sort of picked but we haven't decided anything yet, Billy tell me the truth, is everything ok?"

"Yes Jonny, everything is fine."

Billy didn't sound right, I knew there was something wrong but he wouldn't tell me.

"That's ok mate, I can't wait to see you again, do you think you will be out before Christmas?"

"I don't know Jonny, things are a bit tight, I am getting everything sorted so I can move out but it's looking like about February and to be honest son it couldn't come quicker, I am looking forward to a new beginning."

The tone in Billy's voice worried me but there was nothing I could say or do to help him.

"I will give you a ring in a couple of days mate, I have a lot to do before Karen and the babies get out of hospital."

"No worries Jonny, we will speak soon, give my love to Karen and the kids."

"I will do Billy, take care."

At that I hung the phone up but I was really worried about Billy, it troubled me that I couldn't do anything, I just hoped he was ok.

I drove straight to Buffaloes to make sure everything was sorted but to be honest my stomach thought my throat was cut, I was starving and couldn't wait to get something to eat.

When I arrived the delivery lorry was already half way through our drinks order so Paula was relieved to see me.

"Congratulations Jonny, how's Karen and the babies?"

"Thanks Paula, they are all doing well; it was a long night, Karen is knackered, she will probably sleep for a while today so that's why I nipped out to see if everything was ok."

"Everything is fine, I just panicked that the drinks order hadn't come."

"All sorted then, is Peter about?"

"Yeah, he is in the kitchen."

"Super, I hope there is a big fry up with my name on it?"

"I'm sure he will throw you one up," Paula laughed when she said that, she knew what I was like when it came to a fry up.

I walked into the bar and straight into the kitchen where Peter was doing his prep for the day.

"Hi Peter, how's things going?"

Peter turned, "Hi Jonny, congratulations, everyone ok?"

"Yes mate, everyone is brilliant, any chance you could whip me up a fry up? I am starving!"

"Yeah, no worries Jonny, give me 10 minutes. Go and get a coffee and I will bring it out."

"Perfect Peter, I could eat a horse."

Peter laughed, "No worries Jonny, I will make it large."

I turned and walked out to the bar, got myself a coffee from the machine and took a seat outside at one of the tables. As I sat in the warm sun the previous night's excitement was starting to get to me and I could feel my eyes getting heavy, I must have nodded off as Peter woke me up when he set the biggest fry up I had ever seen down in front of me.

"Get that down you Jonny and then why don't you get your head down for a couple of hours? You look exhausted."

"I am Peter but I have to get back to the hospital."

"I'm sure Karen wouldn't mind if you slept for a couple of hours, you need it."

"You're probably right Peter."

I got stuck into my breakfast/lunch, Peter had sourced out proper soda bread and the sausages he used were from back home too, it was really tasty. It didn't take long to finish and when I mopped up the last of the runny egg with the last bit of soda bread, I carried my cup and plate back into the kitchen and put them into the dish washer. "Thanks Peter, that hit the spot."

"No worries Jonny, glad you enjoyed it."

"Is there anything you need doing today?"

"Yeah Jonny, just for you to go to bed for a couple of hours."

"Think I will Peter, I'm burnt out."

I said my goodbyes and headed for home, as I left the bar a few people had started coming in, I felt bad leaving Peter and Paula to do all the work but I would have been no good to them anyway and they assured me that they didn't mind.

CHAPTER 10

40 Winks

The drive up home seemed to take forever, my eyes were so heavy at one stage I had the music blasting and the windows down just to keep myself awake. I couldn't wait to get home and into bed.

As soon as my head hit the pillow I fell asleep and that's when things started troubling me.

As I lay there sleeping my thoughts and dreams were of back home and Billy and Heather Street; at first it was just a typical night in the bar, Billy and me serving drinks and bantering each other, it was a nice dream but then as I saw myself pulling a pint I heard a familiar voice which made me look up. It was Gerrard standing at the bar with his mop of ginger hair, he said to me, "Why Jonny, why?"

I watched myself stand so still, the look on my face said it all, I was petrified. I walked slowly towards the bar and as I got closer, the look on my face changed, I was screaming. The pint that I had pulled dropped and smashed on the floor as I looked at Gerrard's face, it was half missing, bits of his face were falling to the floor. I looked at Billy who didn't even notice what was happening. I looked at myself standing in front of Gerrard, it didn't add up, it seemed so real but then it was gone, I was standing in front of the bar and Billy was pulling me a pint. He was chatting to me like he didn't know me, I kept asking him, "Billy, it's me Jonny, what's wrong?" but nothing, he didn't even notice me. The more I tried to get his attention the more he ignored me like I wasn't even there, I turned to look around the bar and they were all there Sam, Norman, Jonty, Jason and Paul, they were all drinking and laughing.

I turned back and there was Billy slumped over the bar, I shook him and shook him but he didn't move, I put my head in my hands, I didn't know what to do. I looked up and noticed Billy had a knife in his back, the blood was running onto the bar, I didn't know what to do, I pulled the knife out but the blood starting coming out quicker and quicker. I pressed on Billy's back but I couldn't get the blood to stop, it was now running down the bar and onto the floor. I was screaming for someone to help but nobody moved, nobody came to help, Billy was dead; I removed my hands from his back, they were covered in blood, I turned to face the people in the bar and as I looked at my hands that were dripping with blood I slipped on the blood covered floor and as in seemingly slow motion, I hit the floor.

I woke from my sleep with a jerk, I was soaking with sweat; I jumped out of bed, my heart was racing, I said aloud, "Billy is in trouble, I need to see him."

I walked around the house really worried, was it just a dream or was it a warning? I didn't know what to do so I rang Billy to make sure he was ok, he assured me everything was fine. I told him just to walk away from the bar, just get to Spain, but Billy was a stubborn man and very head strong, you don't work on the Shankill road for thirty years without learning a thing or two. But these where different times on the road now, dangerous times and Sam was struggling to keep the power, especially still being locked away. I think that's why he didn't want to lose his strong hold in Heather Street and the income that he got from all his operations that he ran out of there.

I said my goodbyes and asked Billy to promise me if anything went wrong to ring me, he said he would so I had to just get on with things and hope it was just a bad dream.

I looked at my watch, "Jesus, it's 6 o'clock." I had slept for 3 hours, it seemed like 5 minutes. I got a shower and got a bag together for Karen and the babies, I couldn't wait to get back to the hospital to see them and when I walked into their room Karen was sitting up feeding one of the babies. She was glowing, she smiled as she said to me, "Hiya Love, are you ok?"

Nothing ever seemed to annoy Karen, she was really easy going and she just looked like a natural with one of our babies in her arms, feeding him.

"Yeah love, everything is fine, how are you?"

"I'm a wee bit sore but apart from that I'm ok."

I looked over and our daughter was just lying in her wee cot, happy enough. I went over to speak to her and as she was lying there she was sucking her wee tiny fingers, she was so cute.

"Hello gorgeous and what are we going to call you?" I said as I lifted her.

"Jonny, I was thinking about that, what about Erin? I really like it; it has a ring to it, Erin Andrews."

"Yeah, that's really nice, I like it." I looked at this wee baby I held in my arms and said, "Are you going to be called Erin?" She looked up at me and smiled, I kissed her on the head. "Erin it is then."

"Are you sure Jonny?"

"Yeah Karen, Erin is lovely, she suits it. So what are we going to call this wee one?"

"I was thinking, what about Josh? I quite like it," Karen replied.

"Yeah, that's nice too, I like that as well. So it's settled then, Erin and Josh."

"I am getting out tomorrow Jonny so you will have to be back up here for around 11 or so and make sure you bring the outfits for the babies."

"I am one step ahead of you, they are all here." I pointed over to the corner where I had left the bag with the kids' clothes inside.

"Brilliant Jonny, did you bring me something to change into?"

"Yep, I brought you what you had left out."

"Jonny, don't be worrying about staying to long, the babies are due to go asleep and I know you need to get to Buffaloes."

"It's all sorted, I called in earlier, Paula and Peter has everything under control. I have the rest of today and tomorrow off so don't panic."

"That's great, can you put Erin down and then take Josh and put him in his cot as well?"

"Yeah, no worries love."

I set Erin down so gently into her cot and then did the same with Josh, I stayed for about another hour or so chatting with Karen and then when she was getting really tired I gave her a kiss and told her I would be back in the morning. I headed home as I was shattered as well.

It was another bad night's sleep, I tossed and turned all night, at one point I sat out in the balcony just to cool down and it seemed to work just sitting there in my own thoughts listening to the birds chirp. It really relaxed me so when I went back into bed and I slept for a good couple of hours.

I woke about 9am and had a bit of breakfast, I tided the house up and then left to go and pick Karen and the babies up.

I arrived up at the hospital and Karen and the babies were all ready to go so we just needed to pay the bill and get signed out, which only took about another hour or so.

The next couple of days were hard work and even harder when Karen's mum and dad arrived, our house wasn't big enough, especially in the mornings when I had to get out for work, only having one shower was just not enough. It did take a bit of pressure off me though as Karen's mum was brilliant with the kids, she was a great help the few days that they stayed.

After a couple of weeks we got into a good routine, well, when I say routine it was a case of grab 40 winks when you could, as for sleeping at night - that was hard work. The babies seemed to still be up every 3 hours but you just had to get on with it, I actually enjoyed giving Karen a break in one of the feeds, I took each one in turn out to the balcony and fed them and had a wee chat. It was lovely just to spend that 15 minutes or so with each of them.

CHAPTER 11

The Phone Call

The next few months the babies settled down and slept most of the night; it was really nice on my days off going out for the day and down to the beach and having a picnic, it really was what I looked forward to. I always took a Wednesday off as midweek in the bar wasn't that busy so Paula and Peter were able to manage without me. We had part time staff in the bar now who worked the weekends which were still as busy with all the stag and hen parties, and especially a Sunday afternoon, the bar was always bunged as we had a group on and it was getting a really good name around Benidorm for the place to be at the weekends.

Sunday morning I arrived down at the bar around 8am to open up and clean up from the night before, as I opened the front door the smell of drink hit me, the place was a mess. We had a late one, it must have been 3am when we finally got locked up so I hadn't had much sleep but I was well used to only a few hours kip so it didn't bother me. As I started clearing the tables and putting the glasses into the dish washer, Paula came in, "Morning Jonny, that was mad last night."

"Morning Paula, yeah it was really busy but that's what makes this place work so we can't complain."

"I know Jonny, it was good craic, did you see the state of the stag last night? He was busted."

"I'm not surprised, that big man put away some drink, in fact last night we broke the record over the bar. It was a super night and really fun as well, there really were some headers in last night and the group wasn't bad either."

"Yeah Jonny, it was one of the better nights."

Paula began getting the tables cleaned up and I started restocking the fridges, it only took us a couple of hours and when Peter came at 11 o'clock we were ready to open up. I couldn't believe my eyes when in through the front doors came some of the stag party from the previous night, I was sure that with the amount of drink that they drunk you wouldn't see them again but I was wrong, they went straight into it again and not just a beer, they ordered a round of shots just to start with at 12 o'clock. I got Peter to throw up some grub for them which went down well so when the band came on the bar started filling up. Even better, when there was a downpour of rain later, the punters came rushing in and we had a full party going on.

It didn't cease all day, we had three bands in total on; meeting Roy was a stroke of luck, he made sure that I got the pick of the bands which was hard in

Benidorm as there was so much competition to get the best ones, and I didn't pay over the odds either.

I was able to get a break around six and go for something to eat and to be honest I went to a wee café around the corner just to get my head showered. As I sat there getting stuck into burger and chips my phone rang, I looked at the screen, I didn't recognise the number so when I answered it I was surprised to hear Hammy on the other end.

"Jonny, it's Hammy, are you ok to talk?"

The sound of Hammy's voice worried me.

"Yes Hammy, what's up?"

"It's Billy, he is in hospital."

My heart sunk. "Is he ok Hammy?"

"No Jonny, he isn't, he is on a life support machine."

A huge lump came into my throat, I could hardly answer him.

"Jonny are you still there?" Hammy asked.

"Yes Hammy, I am, what happened, was he in an accident?"

"No Jonny, he was badly beaten up after closing last night, we think it was a robbery went wrong. He is in a bad way Jonny, they had to put him in an induced coma because of the swelling in his brain."

"Oh my God Hammy, I will get a flight home tomorrow, is he going to be ok?"

"Jonny, that's why I'm ringing, they've only given him a 50\50 chance to regain consciousness and even if he does they reckon he will have brain damage so it doesn't look good."

I was numb, I couldn't believe what I was hearing. "Hammy, I will get a flight home tomorrow; can you pick me up from the city airport?"

"Yes Jonny, just ring me when you touch down and I will come and pick you up."

"Thanks Hammy, see you tomorrow."

I hung the phone up and just sat there. I felt really sick and worried that Billy would die, I couldn't even finish my dinner, I took a drink of the ice cold *Coke*, paid my bill and left.

As I walked the short journey back to Buffaloes it seemed like an eternity, the rain was bouncing down and I got absolutely soaked to the skin but as I trenched through the soaked street my mind was focussed on back home. Who could have done this to Billy and more importantly, why?

As I walked through the front doors of Buffaloes the bar was bunged, the noise was deafening and to be honest I couldn't even recognise anyone there. I just walked round to the bar and poured myself a large vodka and drank it, it was only when I set the empty glass on the bar that I felt a hand on my shoulder.

"Joining the party Jonny?"

I looked round and Paula was standing there, I just stood and looked at her and didn't even speak.

"Jonny, are you ok?" she asked.

"It's Billy, he is in a bad way."

"What do you mean Jonny, a bad way? Is he hurt?"

"He's in hospital fighting for his life Paula, it doesn't look good."

"Jonny you need to go home, I will get you a taxi, you're in no state to drive."

"You're right Paula, I do need to go home, but home to Belfast."

I left the bar and got into my car that was parked round the corner and to be honest I couldn't remember the drive home, I just remember parking outside my house. I hadn't even got out of the car when Karen came running down the path, as I stood beside our car she threw her arms round me and was crying, as she sobbed she said to me, "Jonny, I hope Billy is going to be ok, Paula phoned me and told me what has happened."

I hugged her back really tightly, I knew then it wasn't going to be ok but I knew I had to get home and see him.

We walked back into the house and sat down, the kids were in bed so the house was quiet, I just sat with my head in my hands not knowing what to say or do. Karen just sat beside me with her arm round me, we didn't say anything for a good 5 minutes and then I said to Karen, "I will need to book a flight Karen, for tomorrow."

She looked at me, really worried, "Jonny, are you sure it's safe to go back home?"

"Karen, I don't care, I need to see Billy."

"I understand that you need to see him, but what

if something happens to you?"

I looked Karen in the eyes, I wiped a tear away that was running down her cheek, "I need to go Karen, I will be fine."

Karen lifted her phone and booked me a flight, it was for first thing the next morning so we had an early night but to be honest I didn't do much sleeping and neither did Karen. We were up a couple of times with the kids and we just laid in each other's arms for most of the night, I could sense Karen was really worried about me going back to the Shankill Road.

5am and I was up and ready to go, I gave the kids a kiss each on the head and gave Karen a kiss and a hug when I said goodbye.

It didn't take me that long to drive up to Alicante airport, the roads were empty so it was a straight run up with no delays.

As I parked the car in the long stay car park I lifted my bag out of the boot and walked in to get checked in, I looked at the board and saw that the flight was on time so I went and got a bit of breakfast in one of the many outlets.

The next couple of hours dragged by and it was a relief when my flight was called for boarding; I took my seat on the plane and tried to get my head down for a nap but my thoughts were of Billy and to be honest, I was never a religious person, but I prayed for him and hoped he would pull through.

Nearly 3 hours later and I was back in Belfast, as I walked off the plane I turned my phone on and phoned Hammy to come and pick me up.

As I walked through Passport control, the airport security guy sort of delayed looking at my passport. He handed me it back and said, "Enjoy your stay Mr Andrews."

It seemed strange but maybe it was just me being a bit paranoid.

As I walked through the front doors of Belfast City Airport I was greeted with the wind and rain and I said to myself, "Not much changes here does it Jonny?"

I pulled the hood on my jacket up and headed for the drop off and pick up zone which was just across the road.

CHAPTER 12

The Photo

I didn't have to wait long until Hammy arrived, as he pulled up in his motor he looked at me hard, I didn't like the look on his face. I opened the back door of the car and threw my bag in, as I got into the front I said to him, "What's wrong Hammy, you look worried?"

"Nothing Jonny, do you want to go straight to the hospital to see Billy?"

"Yes Hammy, what about him, is there any change?"

"No Jonny, he is just the same."

"Oh right mate."

As we drove down the Sydenham bypass the rain was really heavy and Hammy had to put the window wipers on full just to see the road. We drove past the big yellow cranes in the shipyard and my memories went back to when I was first going out with Karen and the many times I drove down this road. Then I thought of back home, to the Shankill, things were definitely easier back then. We drove up the west link and turned off to the Royal Victoria hospital, as Hammy parked the car the rain eased off a bit.

We walked through the front doors and Hammy said to me, "Jonny, the doctors aren't giving Billy much chance of surviving this, I hadn't the heart to tell you sooner but I don't want you going in here and being shocked at what you see."

I stopped in my tracks and looked at Hammy, "Do you know who did this Hammy?"

"Yes Jonny, it was Sam's crew, it wasn't a robbery. Jonny, he wants you, he knew you would come back home to see Billy and if I told you I would be shot dead, I'm sorry Jonny, you shouldn't have come."

Hammy was a wreck, he sat down on one of the seats and put his head in his hands, he just kept saying he was sorry.

I walked over to him and put my hand on his shoulder, "Hammy, even if you had told me I was coming anyway so don't blame yourself."

He looked up, "Jonny, he is going to kill you."

"Let me worry about that, now come on, let's go and see Billy."

Hammy stood up and wiped a tear from his eye, he genuinely was upset, I had never seen him like this before so I knew what he had told me was the gospel and I needed to be careful.

As we walked into the intensive care unit I dreaded to see what state Billy was in, I held my breath and couldn't believe my eyes when I looked over to a bed in the corner of the room. It was Billy, well, what was left of Billy, he was a mess; he was still unconscious as he was heavily sedated, a tube was down his throat and the machine beside his bed was controlling his breathing. As I got to the side of his bed his injuries were now more clear, his face was a mess, very badly swollen, above his eyes were two large gashes that were stitched, I then noticed a large patch of his head that had been shaved and another large wound that was stitched. As I bent in closer to see it Hammy said to me, "That's where they had to relieve the pressure on Billy's brain."

I looked at Hammy, "He's in a bad way, they are fucking scum bags that have done this."

"I know Jonny, you can't stay here, it's not safe."

"Fuck safe Hammy, I'm going to kill whoever did this."

"Jonny, you have a life far away from here, you should get out of this place as soon as you can."

Just at that a nurse came over, "Excuse me gentlemen, you are going to have to keep it down as these patients need rest."

I hadn't realized how loud I had been talking and when I looked around the room there were three other beds in it with men who were all conscious and had heard everything I and Hammy had said.

"I'm very sorry," I said as I looked at the nurses name tag, "Patricia, I'm sorry for my outburst, I'm just really concerned about Billy, has he made any improvements?"

"No, I'm really sorry but I can't divulge any information, you will have to speak with a doctor."

"And who would that be?" I asked.

"I will ring him and see if he can spare you five minutes."

"Thanks nurse, that would be great."

As she walked over to her desk I turned to Hammy, "We need to talk."

He looked at me, his expression changed in his face. "I know Jonny but not here, there are too many ears and eyes."

I thought to myself, *'Ears and eyes, the good old days.'* "Wait until I speak with the doctor then we will leave."

Patricia came walking back over, "Doctor Beck will be here in five minutes to speak with you."

"Thanks nurse."

I turned to Billy again, I looked him up and down and noticed both his legs were in plaster and one of his arms had pins and was partially in cast as well. "Oh my god Billy, they really have done a number on you." I leant down to the side of his head and whispered into his ear, "Billy, it's Jonny, don't give up keep fighting, just wake up and we will get you sorted, you have a life in Spain waiting on you." I held his hand and I swear he really gently squeezed it, I said again to him, "Just keep fighting mate," and I lightly squeezed his hand back and then let go. I wiped a tear from my eye away quickly and hoped nobody had seen it.

"Hello, how can I help you?" We both turned to see a man in a white coat, he was quite tall with dark hair. "I am Doctor Beck, I am looking after Billy along with a great team of nurses, what do you need to know?"

"Thanks Doctor for coming to speak with us, I just need to know what Billy's chances of surviving this are."

"I'm sorry, I never caught your names," Doctor Beck said.

"This is Hammy and I am Jonny, we are very close friends of Billy."

"Again I have to apologise; I can only divulge that sort of information to immediate family."

Hammy spoke up, "Listen Doctor, Jonny here is like a son to Billy and he has come all the way from Spain to be by his side, he just needs to know if he's going to be ok?"

"Look, I can see you are both really concerned, can you walk with me?" At that the Doctor turned and we followed. As we walked down the corridor Doctor Beck ushered us into a side room away from the main bit of the ward. "Take a seat," he said as he sat down behind a desk, Hammy and I sat on the two seats just opposite him, this didn't look good, I thought. "When Billy was brought in I didn't expect him to last the night, his injuries are severe but it is the trauma on his brain that is the big concern, he has suffered some brain damage and to be brutally honest with you we don't know if he will ever wake up, time will only tell."

"What do you mean Doctor, how long before you will know, a day? Two days? A week? What do you mean?"

"Jonny, we are planning to slowly reduce Billy's medication over the next two days and remove the tube that is helping him to breathe, when we do that we will know the extent of the brain damage."

"What chance do you give him Doctor?"

"Honestly Jonny expect the worse, if he does regain consciousness and does pull through he will probably be bed bound for the rest of his life, the trauma on his brain is over 70 percent." I sat there numb and I didn't know what to say, I was speechless.

Hammy put his arm around me, "Jonny, be positive, Billy is a strong person, if anyone can pull through it's him."

"Hammy be real, Billy won't pull through and to be honest I would rather he never woke up, Billy would never want to spend the rest of his days in a bed getting spoon fed."

"Jonny don't say that, you're just upset."

"Upset? You have no idea Hammy, come on we need to get out of here. Thanks doctor for your honesty, now come on Hammy." At that I stood up and made for the exit door, Hammy followed behind me. After seeing Billy and speaking with Doctor Beck I was now focused and I was fuming at the bastards that did this. I got into the car, nearly taking the door off the hinges as I slammed it, Hammy got in as well.

"Jonny for Christ sake, calm down."

"Oh Hammy I am calm, now you need to tell me everything, what is Sam's plan?"

"I was just told to bring you to Heather Street for 6pm."

"And how were you meant to get me there?"

"Sam knew once you had seen Billy you would go berserk and you would want revenge, I was to tell you that there is a meeting in the club and you were to attend."

"Attend I will, but before I do I need to make a few messages first, take me up the Ballygomartin Road."

"Jonny what are you going to do? What about Karen and the kids?"

I took a deep breath, in my rage I had totally forgot about Karen and the kids and it gave me a wakeup call, I exhaled. "Fuck Hammy, I will have to ring Karen." I lifted my phone out of my pocket and rang Karen.

"Hello love, how's Billy?" she asked.

"Not good Karen, they don't think he is going to pull through."

"Jonny that's terrible, what's going to happen now?"

"I don't know love, it's a waiting game."

"Take as long as you need Jonny, we are ok here, you just be careful and ring me if you need me."

"I will love, give the kids a kiss from me and I will ring you tomorrow."

"Ok, Jonny I love you, hurry home."

"I will love, I love you too."

At that I hung up, we were now driving up the Shankill Road and all the old streets were so familiar;

I had so many memories here, some of them not so good, especially when we drove past the scene of the bomb that I had got caught up in. As we drove past I noticed a plaque and flowers attached to the wall where Frizzell's fish shop used to be, we drove up and round the bend at Woodvale Park and again flowers were attached to the gates but I knew who the flowers were for. We turned left and onto the Ballygomartin Road and headed up towards Springmartin. I got Hammy to stop at the lane and I told him to wait.

As I walked up the lane I had time to think about how this was going to play out but this time I had no answers, I reached the old farm building and what remained of the front door, I paced out 10 yards across the lane and got down on my knees and started scratching at the ground but it was useless. I needed something to dig with as the ground was rock hard, I got up and walked round the old buildings searching for something to dig with, I spent a good 5 minutes looking but there was nothing so I walked back round to the front of the derelict building and there in the long grass I spotted a rusty screw driver. I bent down and picked it up, I looked at it closely and it hit me, this was my screw driver that I had used to kill with, my heart started beating faster and the realization that I was to slip back to my previous life was upon me. I sat on what was left of one of the building's walls and just tried to calm down, as I looked down the lane and over Belfast I said, "Fuck sake Jonny, why? Why can't they just leave me alone?"

I was never going to escape Sam, I should have killed him when I had the chance, I walked across the lane and started stabbing the ground with the screw driver. The hard ground started breaking up, about a foot down I hit my prize, I removed the soil around the box and lifted it out. I set it to the side and refilled the hole back in again, I lifted the box and picked the tape off that sealed it, as I opened the lid I looked inside, I lifted out the plastic bag and threw the tin away. I reached inside and lifted out my gun with the box of bullets, I examined the gun and it was as good as the day I buried it. I opened the box of bullets and loaded the gun, as I stood there holding it I raised it and pointed it down the lane, I said aloud, "You want me Sam Colins, you got me."

I put the box of bullets in my pocket and put the gun down the back of my jeans and pulled my jumper over it. I zipped up my coat and headed back down the lane and to Hammy's car.

As I closed the car door Hammy said to me, "Jonny, there is just one more thing before you go to this meeting, I was told to give you this." He handed me a brown envelope, I was confused.

I looked at Hammy as I took the envelope off him, I said, "What is it?"

"I don't know, I was just told to give you it before I brought you to the club." As Hammy said that he looked at his watch. "Which is now Jonny."

I opened the envelope as Hammy started the car, inside was a photo, I looked at it hard. My eyes were wide open and my heart was thumping out of my chest, I was breathing really fast and heavy, Hammy turned and looked at me. "What is it Jonny?"

I showed him, he said, "Oh my god Jonny."

It was a photograph of Karen pushing our kids in the pram going down our street.

"Fuck," I said. "Bastards." I banged the dashboard with my fist and said, "I'm going to kill these bastards."

CHAPTER 13

The Taste Of Blood

My mind was racing on the short drive down to Heather Street, should I just walk in and shoot whoever was there? If I thought that's where it would end then that's what I should do but I knew it wouldn't end there, they knew where I lived and Karen and the kids were in danger now so I was going to have to sit tight and see what they wanted.

We pulled up outside Heather Street, as Hammy got out of the car I slipped my gun under the front seat along with the box of bullets; I got out and closed the door, as Hammy walked round the front of the car he looked at me, "Jonny, are you ok? I'm so sorry it's come to this but I had no choice, I hope you understand."

"Hammy, if it hadn't happened now it would have happened soon, you and I know Sam won't let go, we will see what they want and just take it from there."

We both walked in through the front doors of the

club, I went first and was greeted by a baseball bat pointed in the middle of my chest. As I looked the guy in the face I didn't recognise him, he was young, about in his early 20s, well built with short hair; he had one distinctive mark on his face, a large scare from just below his eye which ran to his ear, it was quite noticeable. I went to grab the bat but didn't see the other two guys which grabbed both my arms, the guy with the bat lowered it and said, "Now now Jonny, just take it easy, we just want to make sure you aren't carrying."

I sort of struggled a bit but these guys were big lads and had a good grip on me, I was glad then that I left my gun in Hammy's car. I was patted down and then marched forward and put into a chair in front of a table, I was told to put my hands on the table, palms facing up, this worried me a bit but I did it anyway. I looked around to see where Hammy was but he wasn't anywhere to be seen, I asked, "Where is Hammy?"

One of the guys replied, "He wasn't invited to this meeting."

I was worried, a bead of sweat travelled down my forehead and down the side of my face, I lifted one of my hands to wipe it away. Scar face grabbed it and slammed it back down on the table, he shouted at me, "Did I tell you to move, ballbag?"

In one swift move he stabbed a knife through my hand and pinned it to the table, I screamed in pain as I used my other hand to try and remove the knife but he grabbed this hand and again pinned it to the table with another knife, I screamed again.

"Fuck sake, stop," I heard a voice say. "He is here so we can talk, Billy, take a step back."

I looked around I recognised that voice, it was Sam; in that split moment I thought I was going to be killed, I was confused, Sam's here? Why is he still not in Jail?

"What's wrong Jonny, are you surprised to see me?"

I didn't know what to say, the pain in my hands was getting unbearable, I just watched as the blood ran along the table and dripped onto the floor. I was doing my best to stay conscious but I felt sick and dizzy, I gritted my teeth and just stared at him. "What the fuck Sam, what do you want?"

"Oh I have your attention then, well there is the matter of my 70,000 that you took from me, not to mention you killing all my men and then trying to frame me for Jonty's murder." As he said that he grabbed one of the knives and wiggled it, the pain was unbearable, he grabbed the back of my hair and pulled my head backwards. "You have been a really busy boy out in Spain with your bar and nice wee family, you wee cunt."

I winced in pain as he slammed my face into the table, he lifted my head up again, I was semi-conscious, I could feel blood run from my nose and as I tried to stay awake he slammed my face back down into the table hard and knocked me out.

When I came around I was sitting in the corner and my hands were bound together, I was in a lot of pain, I think my nose was broken as well. I could taste blood so I think I must have lost a couple of teeth too.

I looked around and there standing at the bar were the four men, I heard one of them saying, "Just nut the Bastard, we don't need the grief."

My thoughts were of Karen and the kids, I had made a mistake and knew then I shouldn't have came. They came walking over, *'This is it,'* I thought.

"Right Jonny, we own you and your bar, you are working for us now."

I just kept quiet, I knew if I was going to get out of this alive I had to agree to whatever they wanted.

Sam came forward, "Look at me Jonny."

I lifted my bloody face and stared at him, as I sat there in those few seconds I moved my tongue around my mouth, the taste of blood was strong and yep, I think I had about 3 teeth missing. I leant forward and spat a mouthful of blood on the floor, Sam turned to one of his men and said, "Fir fuck sake, will one of you get a cloth to get him cleaned up? Get him a glass of water too to rinse his mouth out."

I just sat and watched as one of them came over, he untied my hands and handed me the cloth and a glass of water. I wiped my face, it was sore, my nose was throbbing but the blood had stopped; as I finished wiping my face another one of them handed me a basin, I took a mouthful of water and swirled it round my mouth and spat into the basin, it was red with the blood and as I took another mouthful the coldness made my now exposed gums hurt. I again spat into the basin, I set the glass down on the table and moved my tongue around my mouth, I felt four gaps and the inside of my mouth was busted too, it was really sore. As I looked at Sam I said, "So what happens now?"

"This is the beginning of you paying your debt back and if you don't then we will give you the choice of who dies."

My heart sunk, I knew what he meant and I knew I had no choice. "So what do you need me to do?"

"Just run on back to Spain, one of my men will call every week for 1000 euros to start with and you will give him a free reign on selling my gear in your bar."

"I couldn't afford 1000 euros a week Sam, that would close the doors."

"That's for you to work the details out, but if you miss one payment then I think you will find that your friends and family will start to go missing. You won't be touched as I want you to see and feel every painstaking part of this, do you understand Jonny?"

"I do understand Sam." As I sat there my mind was racing, I thought to myself, *'How the hell am I going to make this work?'*

I was in a daze when Sam said, "Are we clear about what you need to be doing Jonny?"

I paused and then looked at him, "Crystal."

"Then you can go, but just remember Jonny, you try anything and I will make sure you suffer."

.

CHAPTER 14

An Unexpected Visitor

My mouth was a mess as I got up from the table, my blood soaked hands were throbbing, they needed stitches and I knew I would have to go to hospital. As I walked across the bar I could feel them all look at me but I just focused on the exit door and made a hasty escape.

As I pushed and opened the door the pain travelled up from my hand and I winced, it was really sore but I was glad to see the light of day and to be honest, seeing Hammy sitting in his car was a relief. He turned to look at me and his face said it all, he quickly got out and ran around the front of the car. "Fuck sake Jonny, are you ok?" He put his hand on my shoulder. "This is my fault, I should have told you sooner, I shouldn't have brought you here."

"Hammy, I told you it's not your fault there is only one person to blame and that's that fat bastard in there, he will pay, believe me when I tell you this, when this is over he will not be breathing."

"Jonny just get into the car, if they hear you it will be one in the back of the head."

Hammy opened the car door and helped me inside, as he closed the door I reached under the seat and lifted my gun and box of bullets. I quickly put the gun down the back of my trousers and the bullets in my coat pocket, as he got into the car he said, "Jonny what the fuck did they do to you? Look at your hands, you will need to go to the hospital."

"It could have been worse Hammy, I'm still breathing, take me down to the Mater to get these stitched but I don't want you coming in, you have done enough."

"What do you mean Jonny?"

"You're out Hammy, I don't want you involved in this, you have a wife and kids to think about, if you want my advice…" I turned and looked at him and I really wanted him to listen well to every word I was going to say, "…get as far from the Shankill as you can and never look back, when this starts everyone is a target and Sam won't stop until he gets what he wants."

Hammy gripped the steering wheel, he turned and looked at me, "Jonny, what about Billy?"

I had forgotten about Billy, I exhaled, my head fell backwards, "Fuck! I had forgot about Billy, I don't know Hammy, all we can hope for is that he pulls through but to be honest if I was you I would run away and run far."

"Jonny I don't know, this is fucked up, what does

Sam want?"

"Hammy, just drive and get us out of here."

I didn't want Hammy to know, I didn't know who I could trust anymore, I was on my own but to be honest, that's the way I liked it.

Hammy started the car up, did a three point turn and started heading towards the Mater hospital, as we drove up Cambria Street I clenched my fists to stop the bleeding. The rags that they had given me were now soaked and the pain was getting worse but I had to form a plan and my mind was racing.

"I don't know what I'm doing Jonny, it's a fucking mess."

He turned right onto the Crumlin Road.

"What do you mean Hammy, that it is a mess?"

I looked at Hammy, his tone had changed, he didn't looked worried anymore, in fact he was really calm. He was looking straight ahead when he said, "So how are you going to afford to pay Sam back?"

And there it was, I realised Hammy was working for Sam, he had played me, I gritted my teeth and looked at him hard. "Are you to pick the money up each week?"

Hammy slammed the brakes on and I jolted forward, the car screeched to a halt, he turned to me, "What the fuck do you mean?"

The sound of a car horn made Hammy look out the back window of the car and that was my chance, I reached round with my left hand and grabbed my gun, as I pointed it at his head I said, "Are you working for that fat bastard?"

"No Jonny, I swear, don't shoot."

"How do you know about the money then?"

Hammy paused, I knew then he was working for him, I cocked the gun; as it clicked Hammy moved away and was now leaning against the door, he had his hands up and he begged, "Don't shoot Jonny, please don't shoot, they made me, I had no choice."

The sound of the car horn was really starting to annoy me, "Just fucking drive you turn coat." I lowered my gun and Hammy gripped the steering wheel and off we went, as we drove past Agnes Street I said, "What the fuck Hammy? Was it you who took the photo of Karen and the kids? Was it you who told Sam where I was?"

"No Jonny, I swear I wouldn't do that, I was just told to bring you to Heather Street and hand you the envelope."

"So why do I not believe you then?"

"I don't need you to believe me Jonny, you just have to understand if you don't do what Sam says then you will hurt more than you can ever imagine."

As Hammy said that he was really calm, his voice was very threatening, it was like he was untouchable. I felt like pulling the trigger there and then but knew I couldn't, it would have to wait.

"Just drop me here, pull the fucking car over." I pointed to the Crumlin Road Jail and I pointed my gun at Hammy. "Stop the car."

Hammy stopped the car. "I will be in touch Jonny."

I opened the car door and got out, before I closed the door I crouched down and looked at Hammy, "I never want to see you again, stay away from Billy as well, if I ever see you again you will wish you were never born, do you understand me?"

Hammy just laughed and sped off, the car door slammed shut as the tyres squealed, he nearly hit an oncoming car as it swerved and sounded its horn. I stood up and just watched as he disappeared down the Crumlin Road.

I sat on a wall outside the jail with my gun in my hand, I just stared across the road into thin air, I could see cars going up and down the road but they were just a blur. I hadn't even noticed that it had started raining, I dropped my head and watched the footpath in front of me, drip by drip the blood from my hands hit the ground and I watched as it slowly made its way across the footpath and onto the road. I then noticed the gun I was holding and knew I had to get rid of it if I was going to go to the hospital, I looked round and there just up a wee bit was a thick hedge row so I got up from the wall and walked the short distance. I lifted a plastic bag that had got snagged on one of the many branches and wrapped the gun and box of bullets in it. I shoved it deep into the bottom of the hedge and scrapped some soil and leaves over the bag which made my hands hurt like hell, the rain was really coming down, I was soaked to the skin. As I turned to walk down the road I heard a voice, "Are you alright son?"

I looked up, there in front of me was a wee woman, she had a long coat on, she was slightly hunched over but under the umbrella she held she looked at me with dark piercing eyes. She said again, "Son, are you hurt?"

I held my hands out in front of me, the blood dripped from them, "Aye Mrs, I am just heading to the hospital to get these looked at."

"Come on under my umbrella, I will walk you down son."

I don't know why but I just did what she asked, maybe I just needed someone to talk to or just to walk with; as we walked down the road the wee woman introduced herself, "I'm Lily, what's your name son?"

"It's Jonny."

"And where do live son?"

"I live in Spain."

"So what has you back in Belfast?"

"It's a long story but I came back to see a friend."

"And is that the friend that did this to you?" She held one of my hands, her hand was soft to touch and really warm, she looked up at me, "Jonny, what have they done to you?"

There was something familiar about the way Lily spoke, something soothing, she made me feel at ease.

"I'm ok Lily."

"You're obviously not son, you're in bad way, now come on and we will get you patched up."

As I walked beside Lily under that umbrella walking down the Crumlin Road with the rain pelting down, I felt safe. The pain from my hands was all but gone, the blood had stopped and my mouth wasn't as sore, as we arrived at the entrance of the Mater Hospital, Lily held my hand again. It was really strange but as she squeezed it she said to me, "Jonny Andrews from Broom Street, get all them nasty thoughts out of your head, run away back to Spain and take Karen and the kids far away or you will never be free."

I stood in shock as Lily turned and walked away, pulling her wee shopping cart behind her. I went to call after her but as she hurried across the Crumlin Road, a bus came past and when I stepped forward to shout she was gone, I looked and looked but there was no sign of her.

I stood for a minute or so wondering what had just happened. Who was that wee woman who knew who I was and where I grew up? I turned and I walked through the front doors of the hospital and up to the reception desk, the girl behind the thick glass looked at me as I approached the window. "How can I help you sir?"

I raised my hands, "I need someone to take a look at these."

"Oh my goodness, what happened?"

I didn't know what to say, if I told the truth I would have the peelers on my case and I really didn't want that. "I was in a fight and got bottled"

She looked at me hard, I think she knew I was lying but she just asked, "What's your name and where do you live?"

"John Wright and I live at 18 North Howard Walk."

There was no way I could give my real name, I just hoped she would buy it, as I stood there watching her type my details into the computer she looked up, "I can't seem to find you on the system, have you lived there long?"

"No, I have just moved in last week."

"Oh right, that's why, who is your Doctor?"

"It's Doctor Beck."

She typed that into the computer. "No I still can't seem to find you, we will get you looked at and then get you booked in later."

"Thanks love, that would be great."

"Take a seat and someone will be with you shortly."

I turned and walked to a row of seats against the wall, I was freezing, my clothes were soaked and I just sat and shivered. It wasn't too long before I heard a voice, "John Wright."

I looked up and a Doctor stood in an open door, I stood up and walked over, he showed me inside and pointed to a chair. "Can you take seat here please?" I sat down. "So, you have been in the wars then, can I take a look?" I dropped the blood soaked rags to the floor and showed him my hands. "Turn them over please?" the doctor asked. I turned my hands over, my palms were now facing upwards. "A bottle you said you were attacked with?"

"Yes," I answered hesitantly.

He knew I was telling lies but he never mentioned it, "We will get you cleaned up and then get your hands scanned to see if there is any damage."

"Thanks Doctor."

Over the next hour or so I had my hands cleaned and stitched, they scanned them but there was no long lasting damage.

I walked back to the reception where the girl had some forms that I had to sign and just as I was signing the hospital form, I felt a hand on my shoulder, it startled me. I quickly stood up and turned around. There in front of me was Detective Porter, "I think we need a chat Jonny."

CHAPTER 15

No Way Out

"Porter, what the fuck are you doing here?"

"Never mind me, why are you back in Belfast?"

"I came to see Billy, why is that Bastard Sam not still in jail?"

"Look Jonny, I will explain it all, just give me an hour. Now come on, there are too many eyes in here."

At that he turned and I followed, as we walked through the front doors a car was waiting by the kerb. Porter opened up the back door and as I got in the driver turned and looked at me, I swear he couldn't have been any older than about twenty; he was clean shaven with dark short hair. "Alright Jonny." He said that like he knew me, I thought to myself, 'What the fuck would he know about me?'

"No not really but thanks for asking."

Porter got in the front and we started driving down towards the town. As I sat there in that big car I wondered where they were taking me and what they wanted. Porter turned around, "Jonny, about Sam, the case broke down, evidence went missing and we couldn't hold him."

"What do you mean evidence went missing? You fucking had a body in his garage and a bag of guns, what more did you need?"

"Jonny that was all circumstantial, we had no prints to connect Sam to the gear, the only prints we lifted off them were Jonty's and the garage was in Jonty's name too. Sam just denied it all and the only one that could have given evidence to tie him to it was dead."

I sat there and my heart sunk, he had got off with it and to make it worse he knew everything about me and Karen, I was screwed. "So what happens now?"

"I want you to meet someone Jonny and listen to what he has to say, since you have been away and we couldn't get anything on Sam, there has been developments that we don't like and to be honest the more time goes by, the stronger the grip Sam is getting on Belfast."

"But what has it got to do with me?"

"I just want you to meet this fella, he will explain it better."

We drove for a while then arrived at an army base in Hollywood, it was called Palace Barracks, as we pulled up to the security barrier a soldier carrying a machine gun looked into the car. The driver put his window down, then said the soldier said, "Alright Sir, carry on." The driver thanked him as he put his window up, the soldier signalled to get the barrier raised and we drove in.

As we drove past many buildings, Porter turned and said to me, "Jonny, we will get you cleaned up and a change of clothes before you meet Drew."

I just looked at him, I was totally deflated at the thought of being dragged back into this life again. "Whatever Porter," I replied and just kept looking out the side window as a group of soldiers jogged by.

We pulled up outside what looked like an office block and the driver stopped the car. Porter got out, as did I, the driver got out as well.

I walked slowly behind Porter and the driver who were talking quietly, I couldn't hear what they were saying and to be honest, I didn't care.

As I entered the building, Porter pointed to a side room and said, "Jonny, you will find everything in there you will need to get washed and changed."

"Thanks," I said and walked into the room, closing the door behind me; I stood there looking around the room, there was a table in the corner with what looked like a change of clothes. I went into the bathroom and got undressed, as I stood in front of a mirror that hung over the sink I took a look at myself and just sighed. "Here we go again Jonny, will you ever be free?"

I turned the shower on and stood under the hot water, my face stung as did my hands as I got washed.

I got dried and then put the clothes on that Porter had left for me and left my soaked dirty clothes on the table, as I walked back out to the hallway Porter was standing with a man in a suit, he looked very important. He turned to look at me, he put his hand out to shake mine and introduced himself, "Hello Jonny, I have been looking forward to meet you."

"If you don't mind I will not shake your hand as mine is still a bit sore."

I showed him my hand and he said, "Don't worry Jonny, my name is Drew, I have a problem and think you could be the solution."

We walked down the corridor and into a room that overlooked a football pitch, we sat near the window, on the table was tea and coffee. Porter asked me if I would like any but I refused, I just wanted to know what the hell was going on.

"Jonny, I will just get to the point," Drew said. "We know you are doing well for yourself out in Spain but things haven't changed back here, have they?"

"No they haven't and I have been pushed into a corner, that bastard Sam will never let go, I should have killed him when I had the chance, now he is threatening my family and I fear he will carry the threats out."

"That's why I think we can help each other, look Jonny, I am the head of a unit that works below the radar, if you know what I mean?"

"No actually, I don't know what you mean."

"It's like this, we have problems all over the world and sometimes those problems need dealing with without the courts getting involved."

"So why is that my problem?"

"It's not your problem, the only problem you have is Sam and to be honest he is starting to get involved in things that has got the attention of my unit, and that's where you come in."

"What do you mean Drew?"

"We have information that Sam has a contact in Spain that is going to supply him with guns and explosives."

"If what you tell me is true then what has it got to do with me?" I asked again.

"We need you to take this guy out, our last attempt failed and we lost our agent in Spain and when Porter told me that you had worked with him before I knew it was you we want."

I turned to Porter, "What the fuck Porter? Is this fucking James Bond?"

"Something like that Jonny," he replied.

I turned to face Drew, "So what happens now?"

"We are going to get you back to Spain, you will be contacted with details of your target and where to get him, the reason why we want you is that you know the area where our target is and we know you are quite capable of doing the job."

"So what is in it for me?"

"We will take Sam out and you and your family will not have to worry about him again."

"But Sam already has things in place, he is to collect a thousand euro a week off me and is to take over my bar, so he has men out there in place already watching my family."

"We already know that Jonny, as soon as we get our man then you can take out the rest of Sam's men in Spain, we will take care of the rest."

'This is a bloody nightmare,' I thought. *'What the hell am I getting involved in? I just want to get home.'*

Drew reached under the table and pulled out a bag, as he handed it to me he said, "Jonny, there is everything you need in here to keep you going until you get back to Spain, we have booked you into a hotel up at the international airport." As he reached into the bag he pulled out a brown envelope, he opened it and emptied the contents onto the table, there was a mobile phone, a passport, car keys and a bank card. He handed the phone to me and said, "This is how I and only I will contact you, the number will be withheld but when you hear the phrase operation 'Life's a beach' you will know it's me. Now here is your new identity, only use it when flying in and out of Spain and when you need money, there is 10 grand in an account so that will help to keep Sam off your back until the job is done. There is a car parked in Alicante Airport level two and it is parked in bay 54, always leave it there when you're finished. Everything you need is in the boot, I take it you haven't lost your touch with a hand gun?"

I just looked at Drew, this was going too fast, was I now becoming an agent for them, a hired killer? "Look Drew I just want this finished, I will take your target out in Spain if it means I am free of this nightmare but I want to be the one to pull the trigger on Sam so I know for sure it's over and after that I want to be left alone to raise my kids in peace."

"Of course Jonny, I understand that you want him dead, we will set it up as soon as our target in Spain is executed but both targets will have to be taken out within 24 hours of each other if it's to work."

"Why?" I asked.

"Because if Sam finds out that we have taken out his contact in Spain he will know that he will be next and he will go underground and we will never get him."

"I still want to be the one to kill him."

"Then we will do it in 2 weeks today, that will give you time to get set in Spain."

"One more thing, I need to know if Billy is going to be ok."

Porter turned to me, I didn't like the look on his face. "Jonny I am so sorry, Billy suffered a massive heart attack, he didn't make it son."

I didn't know what to say, I just stared at him, I couldn't believe Billy was dead. Porter reached out and put his hand on my shoulder, "Jonny I'm so sorry, I know you and Billy were close."

I looked at him. "Billy is dead?" I asked as my eyes filled with tears.

"Yes Jonny, he is."

I wiped a tear from my cheek and gritted my teeth, I took a deep breath and said, "Then it's definitely me that is going to end this, I want that Bastard Sam dead. Drew, I am your man for the job, I want this done as much as you so let's get started."

"I'm glad Jonny and I know you won't let me

down."

Porter and I left, he drove me up to a Hotel at the International airport, we didn't talk much, I just sat in my own thoughts and thinking of Billy. We drove up the motorway and towards the Hotel, as I got out of his car he said, "Good luck Jonny, I hope this all works out for you."

I just slammed the door and I walked into the hotel, I booked in and went straight to my room and as I walked into the room I threw my bag on the floor and fell onto the bed and just stared at the ceiling. Karen came into my thoughts and I knew I would have to ring her and let her know about Billy, but I could never tell her I was working for a secret unit within the government.

CHAPTER 16

Bide My Time

I laid for a while before I made the dreaded phone call.

"Hi love, how's you?"

"Never mind me, why have you not rang me before this?"

I knew by Karen's tone she wasn't pleased with me but I had no answers, the last couple of days were a nightmare so I just blurted it out, "Billy is dead Karen, he's dead," as I spoke, a tear ran down my cheek.

"Jonny, what happened?"

"He had a heart attack."

"I'm so sorry Jonny, when is the funeral?"

"I don't Know Karen but I can't stay, I'm up at the Airport in a Hotel, my flight is first thing in the morning."

"Jonny what's wrong, why can't you stay?"

"It's complicated, I just can't stay."

"Jonny, what do you mean?"

"It's Sam Karen, he Isn't in Jail and it's not safe for me here."

"Oh my God Jonny, just get home."

"I am Karen, I should be home by about 3pm tomorrow."

"Ok love just stay in the Hotel until you have to go for your flight, promise me you won't leave until then?"

"I will Love, I'm shattered, I'm just going to go to bed."

"Ok Love, ring me in the morning."

"I will."

At that I hung up, it was killing me that I couldn't tell Karen the truth but what else could I do? I was leading a double life again.

I lifted the Passport out of my bag and opened it up, when I got to the page with my photo on it I read the name out loud - Scott Fraser. I smiled as I said it, "Scott Fraser, sounds good Jonny Boy."

Holy shit, I was really doing this, I lifted the bank card out which had a piece of paper stuck to it. The paper had a number wrote on it, '1402 account password', I then lifted the keys they had four circles inscribed on them and the word Audi. This was a nice car, I thought and I wondered what colour and make it was. I set the stuff along with the mobile phone on my bedside table and got undressed, I got into bed and to be honest I didn't sleep much but I knew it was the safest place I could be.

The next morning, I got up early around 6am, my flight was at 9.40am so I had plenty of time to get breakfast and get to the Airport.

As I sat in the Hotel dining room I struggled to use the knife and fork to eat my breakfast, my hands were really sore and I winced a couple of times with the pain of them. The girl that served me came over, "Are you ok sir, can I get you anything?"

"If you could can I get a couple of pain killers? My hands are really sore."

"That's not a problem, I will be back shortly." She turned and walked off and I got back to trying to eat my fry up. When she returned she handed me two tablets, "I think these will do the trick for you."

"Thanks very much," I replied and I threw the tablets in my mouth and washed them down with a gulp of tea.

"Is there anything else you need sir?" the girl asked.

"Yeah there is, could you order me a taxi please?"

"Yes, where are you going?"

"Over to the airport," I replied.

The look on the girl's face changed, she smiled as she said, "You're joking aren't you?"

"Why?" I asked.

"You could walk to the airport in 10 minutes from here."

As I looked out the window I replied, "In this weather I don't think so, I have had enough of getting soaked, I can't wait to get home to Spain."

"Seriously, do you live in Spain?"

"Yeah I do, just outside Benidorm."

"Oh, you're so lucky, I would love to live in Spain."

I just smiled and replied, "So could you get me a taxi?"

"Yes, what time would you like it for?"

I looked at my watch, it read 6.30. "Could you book it for 7 please?"

"Yes of course I could." She walked off and I finished my breakfast, I went back to my room and packed my stuff, as I put my coat on the phone rang on the bedside table, I lifted it.

"Hello Mr Fraser, your taxi is outside."

"Thanks very much, I'm coming now."

I left the room and walked down to reception where the receptionist told me my room was pre-paid and to have a nice day, I thanked her and left.

It really was chucking down so I was glad to get into the taxi and make the short journey to the airport where my flight was on time. As I checked in and got through the security I started feeling a bit funny, my head was a bit light and I needed to sit down.

As I sat trying to get myself together I realised that the tablets the girl had given me must of been to strong cause I felt drunk, I sat for about 5 minutes but I then started feeling sick so I sort of staggered to the nearby toilet. As I got into one of the cubicles I boked everywhere, most of it hit the toilet but some went all over the floor. I really did empty my stomach and as I stared down the toilet I noticed parts of my breakfast but I also saw the remains of the tablets I had taken.

I stood up and got my balance, if I didn't know any better I swore I was drunk, I lifted my bag and I walked over to the basins. As I set my bag on the floor I turned the cold water tap on and cupped my hands under it, the cold water eased the pain in my hands and as I threw the water over my face it made me feel a lot better, I repeated this a couple of times and then lifted a couple of paper towels out of the machine on the wall and dried my hands and face.

I went back out to the Airport departure lounge and sat over a cup of coffee and waited for my flight to be called.

At 9.10 I was called to board the plane and as I sat in my seat I couldn't wait for it to take off and leave N. Ireland.

I must have fell asleep on the plane because the next thing I knew we were getting ready to land in Alicante and as I looked out the window the bright blue skies and hot sun made me realise I was home.

It didn't take long to get through the Airport and I went straight to level two in the car park and bay 54 to see what car they had left me. As I stood in front of it I was chuffed, it was a black Audi A5 and it had all its windows tinted out. I lifted the keys out of my pocket and opened it up, I went into the boot to see what gear Drew had given me and as I looked inside I just stood with my mouth wide open. There was three different guns but the one that caught my eye had a silencer attached to it, I looked around the car park to see if anyone was about but it was clear so I lifted the gun to have a closer look. It was not so heavy but it was a smasher, a real piece of equipment, I set it back in the boot and plundered a bit further into the bag. I lifted out a brown envelope and looked inside, it had a couple of photos and a file with a name Mick Cullen wrote on the front of it, as I looked at one of the photos which had 4 men standing in it, one of them had his face circled in a blue marker and the word beside it read TARGET.

I realised this was the guy I had to take out so I opened the file and read it to find out a bit more about him, I decided to get into the car so I wouldn't look so suspicious.

As I sat in the front seat, the car was beautiful, all leather interior, really low to the ground and I couldn't help myself, I had to start it. What a beast of a car this was, it roared like a lion, it really was a high end motor.

I turned the engine off and sat and read Mick's file, it had all his movements and who his contacts were and when I came across one of the names my heart sunk, it was Roy Greer who I had become friends with. This was getting complicated but it didn't say how he knew him so I just hoped it was through the entertainment business and nothing more.

As I sat there reading, the mobile phone rang, I lifted it and answered, "Hello."

"Operation life's a beach."

"Hello Drew."

"Don't use names, just listen, I take it you're back in Spain, did you get the file?"

"Yes, I am sitting reading it now."

"So you know your mark then?"

"Yes, I know who I have to take out but I will need time to find him."

"Just settle back home for a couple of days and I will be in contact with more information."

"Will do." At that Drew hung up and I threw the phone in my bag.

I sat for a few more minutes reading through the file but there was nothing more of interest to me, I knew what had to be done. I just needed to get a plan together and it needed to be tight, no mistakes because I was dealing with high end criminals, not just corner boys from the Shankill Road.

I put the file back in the boot and locked the car, I walked to the lift and I went up to level 4 where I had parked my car. I opened the boot and threw my bag in, I got in and started it up, I always thought I had a nice car but when I sat In the Audi I knew my car was just a bog standard motor. To be honest though, I would rather have this life than the one I was now on the road towards.

I drove out of the airport and headed for home, Karen and the kids were in my thoughts but it was how I was going to explain my hands and face to Karen that was going to be the hard part.

I took my time driving home, it took me about 45 minutes but when I eventually pulled up outside our house Karen and the kids where in the garden under a big umbrella playing on the grass. They looked so happy and for a split moment so was I, but then the look on Karen's face said it all as she looked on in horror while I locked the car and walked towards the house. She ran out of the garden and threw her arms around me, "Oh my god Jonny, what happened?"

I just hugged her for a few seconds as she was upset and then I told her, "I told you Sam wasn't in jail and this is his handy work."

I showed her my hands and she cried but through the tears she said, "We have to run away Jonny, we have to go far."

"Karen, he will always be out there no matter where we go, he will always be looking for me, come inside so I can explain to you what is going to happen."

I took Karen by the hand and we walked into the garden, we lifted our kids and walked into the house where we sat in the living room.

"Listen, the only reason I'm back here alive is that I agreed to pay Sam 1000 euro a week."

"Jonny, I don't care how much he wants, we have to run away."

"Karen, we can't, he has someone watching us, we have to just do what he asks."

Karen held her head in her hands and cried, "Jonny, what are we going to do?" she said through her tears.

I put my arm around her, "It will be ok Karen, I will get it sorted, we will get through this."

"I hope so Jonny, I really hope so."

I just held Karen in my arms for a few minutes just

to reassure her that we would be ok.

I lifted Josh who was starting to get unsettled, he really was getting big and as I walked out to the garden I gave him a kiss on the cheek. "How's my wee mate?" I said as I sat on one of the seats. He smiled at me, the slabbers were dripping off his chin as he was teething so I wiped his chin with his bib. He nearly ate the hand off me and I said, "Are you hungry wee man? Will we get you a wee jar of food?" I swear he could understand me as he chuckled as he was biting on his hand, I walked back into the house and put him into his high chair. I turned to Karen who still had tears in her eyes, "Does Erin need fed too love?"

She looked up at me, "Jonny, how can you just be so calm?"

I wasn't going to tell her what was planned, she really didn't need to know. "I told you, we will be fine, we just have to get on with living love."

"But how can you be so calm about it Jonny?"

"Because we have no other choice, we will just have to find the 1000 euro a week and pay him."

Josh was getting a bit fed up in his chair, he was hungry and starting to cry.

"Should we get you fed son?" I said to him as I went and got a jar out of the cupboard and put it into a dish and heated it up; as I stirred it walking over to where he sat I tried a bit of it and to be honest, it was quite nice. I sat in front of him as Karen put Erin in the other high chair and I started feeding them both, Erin was brilliant to feed, she was as good as gold but your man here was a nightmare, he spat it out, rubbed his hands in it and of course rubbed it all over his face and hair. By the time we finished he was covered from head to toe and it was the bath for him, he was just a typical wee boy.

I reassured Karen that we would be ok and that the bar could still survive even whilst paying Sam, she wasn't so sure but then she didn't know about the deal I had with Drew and becoming an agent for MI6.

After dinner, I headed down to Buffaloes to make sure everything was running ok and to let Paula and Peter know that I was back, as I parked the car and made the short walk to the bar I was stopped by a guy on a motorbike. He pulled right up in front of me and I knew he was the contact for Sam, as he turned the bike off he raised the visor on his helmet, "Jonny Andrews I presume?"

"Yeah it is, why do you ask?" as if I didn't know what was coming.

"I am working for Sam and just to let you know I will be collecting his money on Friday at 9pm, so have it ready for me."

He was really aggressive and just typical of the type of guy Sam always had about him, plenty of muscle but not much brains.

"Yep, I will have his money."

"Make sure you do," he replied as he started his bike up and sped off, leaving me standing there. I just shook my head and said, "And so it begins."

I walked on round to the bar where it was really busy, Paula had everything going like clockwork, she really was a good manager and if anything we had to keep the bar running no matter what.

"Hi Jonny, what the hell happened to you?"

"It's a long story Paula but nothing to worry about, I'm just glad to be back, what needs doing?" I just wanted to deflect the conversation, I didn't want anyone else knowing what had happened and what was going to happen.

"Jonny everything is fine, just go home, you don't need to worry. Go home and get some rest."

"No Paula, I need to get back to work, I need to keep busy."

"Ok, could you restock the bar? I think it is getting a bit low on bottled beer."

"I can do that."

I went straight into the old routine and I liked the simplicity that it was, no distractions, and just got on with it.

It was around 11pm when the place was absolutely crammed, the DJ was super and the crowd was buzzing. I helped out behind the bar and the drink was flying, but one of the guys in the bar caught my eye, he just didn't look like he was with anyone so I watched him for a while and I noticed he was going in and out of the toilet a lot. At about 11.45 I approached him, he was about the same height as me but well-built, he was wearing a pair of jeans and a black skin tight t-shirt, he had grey short hair and had both his arms tattooed.

"Can you tell me what you are doing?" I asked him.

"What the fuck has it got to do with you?"

"Will this is my bar, and watch your tone with me or you're out."

"I work for Sam and I only answer to him so you just fuck away off behind the bar and keep pulling pints."

My blood was boiling, my bar was being taken over and I couldn't do anything about it, I just had to bide my time and bite my lip.

I walked away, I knew he was selling drugs and Sam was tightening his grip on my bar, *'On my bar!'* I thought. "I can't wait to get started," I said under my breath as I walked back behind the bar.

The rest of the night I kept watching him, he didn't leave until near 1am and the absolute brass neck of him, he winked at me as he walked past the bar. I just gritted my teeth and said nothing.

CHAPTER 17

Regular As Clockwork

The next couple of days I spent more time with Karen and the kids during the day and worked the late shift in the bar. Every night around the same time your man came in and peddled his gear, the atmosphere in the bar was different and the takings went down a bit as well so I knew the drugs were taking over. I also knew I had to go with the flow.

Friday afternoon around 12.30pm I went to the bank to lift Sam out his 1000 euro, as Scott Fraser, I gave the girl the bank card and my passport and it went really smoothly, no questions asked. She was really pleasant and helpful, she wanted me to meet the manager but I put her off and said I had no time and would arrange a meeting on a different day. I left and went for a bit of lunch in one of the back street cafés, just to get my head showered.

As I sat there enjoying a bowl of soup and a sandwich a big flash car pulled up outside, it was the car that caught my eye, it was a top of the range silver BMW and it had all its windows blacked out. As it parked alongside the kerb, an extremely large man in a suit got out of the front passenger side, he was built like a brick shithouse. He opened the back door and an elderly well-dressed man got out also wearing a suit, he was of heavy build too but not muscle, just fat. He wasn't that tall but was very distinguished looking with grey short hair and he was draped in gold, his hands were huge and he wore rings on every finger, but it was the tattoo that I noticed: it was a hand gun and it covered one side of his neck. My eyes widened as I recognised him, it was Mick Cullen, my target; he walked into the café and sat at a table just inside the door behind me, his minder walked round the café and into the toilet where he came out within a few seconds. He then walked over to the BMW opened the passenger door and I overheard him say, "Come back in an hour." He closed the door and the car drove off, he then returned to where Mick was sitting and sat beside him, He lifted a paper and started reading it.

As for Mick, he had his nose stuck in the menu and when the girl came down to take his order I heard her say, "Are you going for something different today Mick or is it just your usual?"

My ears pricked up on his reply, "I think I will just have my usual," it was the way that he spoke that I noticed he was from Ireland, he had a real strong Irish accent and as he handed her the menu back we exchanged a glance. I lifted my sandwich and took a bite, my heart was thumping, I struggled to keep my cool. Every bite of that sandwich was a struggle to swallow but I knew I had to stay and listen for anything that I could use in my plan to kill him. I slowed down eating just trying to make it last as long as I could and when I did finish my lunch, I ordered a coffee. I got up and walked slowly past where Mick and his minder were sitting, they didn't notice me at all, Mick was shovelling a really large portion of lasagne into his gob, I swear he was eating like a big fat pig, his mouth was plastered in sauce and it didn't even annoy him. As for the minder, he was marking horses out on his paper so I was invisible to them, which is what I needed.

I walked into the toilet which had three urinals along a wall and then opposite were two cubicles, along the other wall were two sinks and above the sinks was a window which was about two foot square with frosted glass. I noticed that there were steel bars on the outside of the window to secure it. I looked around a bit more and then had a piss, I washed my hands and as I dried them under the hand drier the door opened and Mick's minder walked in. He walked straight to the cubicles, opened both doors and then looked at me and walked out again, as I finished drying my hands and walked out he was standing right outside the door. I slowly walked past him wondering why he was still there and then the penny dropped, as he nodded over to Mick he got up from the table and went to the toilet, it was that moment my plan was hatched. I sat at my table drinking my coffee with a slight smile on my face, I looked at my watch: 2.05pm, both Mick and his minder returned to their table and sat and finished their drinks. It was around 2.15pm when the BMW returned and Mick and his minder got up from their table, the girl walked over to him and said, "See you tomorrow Mick."

He replied, "You will love."

They got into the BMW and left, I finished my coffee and paid my bill and left to go to the bar.

All night I planned how to get close enough to kill Mick, but how to get away without having a shootout with his minder was the main part of the plan that would take a bit of thinking. It was now 9pm and the bar was getting busy, as I was clearing a few tables I felt a hand on my shoulder, I turned to find a young lad standing in front of me, he must have been no more than about 23. I asked him, "Can I help you?"

"Indeed you can, I believe you have an envelope for Sam."

It was the guy on the motorbike and he was here for the 1000 euro, I looked at him hard, if there was one thing I was good at it was never forgetting a face, especially the ones that made my life hell. I reached into my jeans' pocket and lifted out the folded envelope with the money in, as I handed it to him he said, "Now that wasn't too hard, see you next week, same time, same channel."

He laughed as he said that and walked out, I thought to myself, *'You arrogant fucker, you won't be laughing when this is over.'*

Again around 11pm the other guy came in to sell his drugs, he pushed past me and had a smirk on his face. He was building up quite a trade as over the next couple of hours the toilet door might as well have been a revolving door as it never stopped. The amount of young people that were out of their heads was unbelievable, at one point all we were selling over the bar was water and *Red Bull*. It was then that Paula said to me, "Jonny, we need to have a word."

"I know Paula, I know what you're going to say."

"The DRUGS Jonny, the place is rife with them."

"I know Paula but my hands are tied, there is nothing I can do, we will just have to ride this out for a while."

"It will close us down Jonny, if we don't get the trade over the bar then we are screwed."

"We will look at it tomorrow and try and work something out, can you meet me in the morning early around 8.30am?"

"Yes Jonny I can, should I tell Peter to come as well?"

"No, I don't want him involved, the less he knows the better."

"Ok Jonny but I hope you can get this sorted."

"So do I Paula."

We closed up around 2am and as I drove home my thoughts were of Mick and Sam and how I needed this done, and quickly.

The next morning I met Paula in the bar, we sat at a table that I had cleared and we had a coffee each.

"Listen Paula, if I could tell you I would but the less you know about why someone is selling drugs in the bar, the better. "

"Stop talking crap Jonny, it has to stop. You don't understand, your bar will close if you don't get it stopped, I have seen it all before, it will only take a row to break out and the bar will be trashed then the Policia will close you down. Even worse, if they find out that drugs are being sold here they will throw you in jail and your bar will be closed for a long time."

"That's all well and good Paula but how do we stop it?"

"I have a friend who will take whoever is selling the drugs outside and break his legs, that should stop it."

"Trust me Paula, that will only make it worse, I will deal with it. More importantly, we need to look at the takings over the bar, if it is only water and *Red Bull* that we are selling late on then we will just charge a stupid price for it."

"Like how much Jonny?"

"Charge them 5 euro each, that should bring the takings up."

"Well you're the boss Jonny and it's your call."

"Who is the fella you know that can handle himself?"

"I used to date him a while back, it didn't work out but we stayed friends, he is a bouncer in one of the nightclubs."

"Could you give him a ring? I would like to meet him."

"Yeah Jonny, when and where do you want to meet?"

"Do you know the wee café that is at the end of Aveda de Castellon right on the corner of the Promenade?"

"Yes I do, they make a lovely sandwich in there."

"That's the one, could you get him to meet me for lunch around 1pm?"

"Yeah, yeah, I will give him a ring now."

"Thanks Paula."

I lifted our two empty cups and brought them into the kitchen, as I walked back out Peter had just came in.

"Hi Peter, how's it going?"

"All good Jonny, how's things with you?"

"Just the usual Peter, stressed out."

"Sorry to hear about your mate Billy."

"Thanks Peter, I will miss him a lot."

"How's Karen and the kids?"

"They are doing ok mate, getting big."

"I know Jonny, they don't stay babies too long, before you know it they will be starting school."

"You're right there Peter, time is flying by."

"I will need to do a run to the cash and carry, we need a few things."

"No worries Peter just put it on the account as usual."

"Speaking of that Jonny, you need to give me a cheque, the girl in the accounts wants a payment."

"Yeah, yeah Peter, how much do you need?"

"850 euro."

"That's ok, I will go and get the cheque book."

"Thanks," Peter replied as he walked into the kitchen.

I went into the office and into the safe to get Peter a cheque, on my return to the bar Paula told me that her mate was ok to meet me at 1pm.

I gave Peter the cheque and then started stocking the bar and cleaning up, it wasn't long before the first punters arrived for breakfast. Peter's special was always asked for: 2 sausage, 2 bacon, 2 eggs with toast and free tea or coffee all for 4 euro, you couldn't beat it with a big stick. We always had around 30 to 40 in for breakfast and it put the morning in quickly, it was always the same routine, by 12pm we had a guy come in to do a set till 2pm, nothing too mad just background music but it seemed to draw a lot of people in. Peter's menu was always really good, he really was a good chef and knew his stuff. I disappeared around 12.45 to go and meet Harry the bouncer just when the part time staff arrived, we now had 10 staff and it gave me the opportunity to have time off.

As I arrived at the back street café around 1pm I was met by a real tough looking guy, he must have been 6ft 2" tall, not a piece of fat on him and really well built. He was dressed in a pair of tracksuit bottoms and a skin tight white t-shirt, he really looked tough as nails and somebody that you wouldn't mess with.

"You must be Harry," I said as I put my hand out.

"Yes I am and you must be Jonny, Paula has told me all about your problem."

"Come and sit down for lunch and we will have a chat."

"Oh right, ok," Harry replied.

We sat at the same table that I sat at the previous time I was here, it had a good viewing point and when I say that, I mean to keep an eye on Mick if he arrives.

"What would you like to eat?" I asked Harry.

"Just a sandwich and a coffee would do me."

"Yeah, think I will have the same."

As the girl came down to take our order the flashy BMW pulled up outside. As I watched on it was the same routine, the minder got out, opened up the back door and out stepped Mick, they walked in and as Mick sat at the same table about 10 feet from me, the minder walked round and checked the café over.

"Are you ok Jonny, you have went a bit quiet?" Harry asked.

"Oh right, sorry Harry, I was admiring that car, it's really nice."

"Yeah it's a nice motor, but back to the business in hand, what do you need me for?"

"I would like you to come and run the security in my bar."

"But I have a cushy deal where I am now, what would make me want to give that up?"

"As always - money Harry, how much are they paying you?"

"For the 4 nights I work there I get 400 euro in my hand."

I took a breath, *'That's good money,'* I thought. "What if I was to match it, would you be interested?"

"Not really Jonny, I like the place and there is not much hassle."

"What about less hours but the same money?"

"What are you talking?"

"I would need you Friday, Saturday and Sunday from around 9pm till closing, which is usually around 2am."

"Sounds good but what about your drugs problem?"

"We need to leave it as it is for another 2 weeks and then we will get it sorted."

Harry put his hand out, "Then I'm your man, when do you want me to start?"

"Next Friday will be perfect, can you meet around 9pm?"

"Yes, that will be fine."

"Ah good timing, here's lunch."

The girl set our plates down and then another girl set our coffee down.

"I hope they taste as good as they look Jonny."

"Oh they do Harry," I said as I got wired in to one of them. As we sat eating I kept a close eye on Mick and I was chuffed to bits when he kept to his same routine, he stuffed his lunch into his bake then the minder went and checked the toilets before Mick went to the toilet and then the BMW arrived to pick him up. While he was leaving I looked at my watch: 2pm, and he was like clockwork. Harry and I finished our lunch and we said our goodbyes, I knew then this is where I was going to kill Mick.

As I walked back to Buffaloes my phone rang, "Operation life's a beach," Drew said.

"Hello, I am all set, I have my mark in place and am good to go in 4 days."

"There has been a development, your second target is on route and will be arriving on Wednesday, you will have to abort until he returns back."

"No, I will deal with both when he arrives, I will just have to take them both out."

"It's your call but make it clean, no mistakes, there is too much to risk. If this deal gets done then lives will be lost."

"I understand that, there won't be any mistakes, I assure you."

"Ok, if you take both out then there will be another 20,000 euro placed in your account."

"What about the motor, do I get to keep it?"

"Yes, the motor is yours, just make sure both targets are taken out."

At that Drew hung up, to be honest I chanced my arm with the motor but was chuffed at my new wheels and the payment I was getting. I was beginning to like being Scott Fraser, but most of all I was excited to get the chance to execute Sam once and for all.

I doubled back and around the back of the café, I found where the bathroom window was and had a good look at the bars on the window, they were built into a frame which was screwed to the frame of the window. I gave a couple of tugs on them and they seemed loose, they must have been there for years as the frame of the window had rotted and the bars were barely being held in place. I had a good look at the window, the glass wasn't that thick and would be easily broken so I knew what I needed to do, it was just a case of timing.

I wandered back to Buffaloes and told Peter and Paula about bringing security on board for the weekends, with it being a Tuesday I was able to leave them to it and head home.

Karen, I and the kids had a wee evening round at the pool, the kids really loved the water. It was really relaxing away from the all my worries and the hustle and bustle of Buffaloes. While we were in the pool with the kids Karen said to me, "How was work today love?"

"Just the usual, I have hired security for the weekends, I think it's time we were a wee bit more conscious about who is coming into the bar."

"Yeah I think you're right, who is it?"

"A fella called Harry, Paula knows him."

"Oh right, that's good, I would feel better knowing that there is someone else to deal with the head cases and not just you."

"You wouldn't mess with this guy, he is an animal."

Josh started laughing as I dipped him in an out of the water, Erin loved the water as well when Karen did the same. It really was a lovely evening, the sun was nice and warm and the kids were good as gold, it tired the them both out and by 9pm they were in bed and sleeping which gave Karen and me time on our own. It was then that Karen wanted to talk about

Billy and what had happened with Sam, "Jonny, Sam won't stop will he?"

"No Karen, he won't, but as long as he gets his money we are safe. That's what drives him so stop worrying, we will be ok."

"But Jonny what if it's not just the money he wants, what if he wants revenge?"

"Listen love, if he comes for me I will deal with it, we aren't back on the Shankill where he is protected. To be honest, I would love it if he had the balls to come for me."

"Stop talking like that Jonny, we have kids to worry about."

"And that's exactly why I would take him out, for us to be free."

"But what if something happens to you, what would I do?"

"Don't think like that, nothing is going to happen, as long as he gets his money then we are fine."

"I hope you're right Jonny, I really do."

Karen was really worried, but if only she knew that this would be over in three days.

"Would you like a cup of tea love?" I asked to change the subject.

"What, you making me a cup of tea? Are you feeling ok?"

"You're a laugh a minute," I replied, smiling.

"Yeah, I would love one."

"Do you want some toast as well?"

"That would be lovely, with loads of butter."

"You read my mind," I replied.

After we had our supper we both went to bed as I think it was a long day for both of us.

The kids had us up early the next morning and it was the usual routine, a bit of breakfast then I headed over to work to get things sorted, but most of all to put the final bits in place for my plan to execute Mick and Sam.

I got a couple of items that I needed to finish my plan and I was set, it was just a matter of putting the time in now. The morning up in work was busy, we had a drinks order that needed hand balled in, I didn't mind this as it kept me busy and my mind off killing again. I had to do one last survey of the café to make sure Mick was there at the same time and did the same things at the same time and yep, bingo, he was as regular as clockwork. So I was set, everything was ready for the next day when Sam was due to arrive and I was certain the meeting would be here in the café over lunch.

CHAPTER 18

Out Of Order

Later on that evening I went around the back of the café and made sure the bars on the window were taken out and just set back in place. I took a walk round the streets that were close by to decide my best route to get away, as I walked up one street and down the next I decide the best place to park my car so it would be easy to disappear into the traffic and make sure of my escape.

I had everything in place and with it being a Monday I helped out in the bar, it was Karaoke night so there was a good crowd in and to be honest there were some half decent singers. It was really busy over the bar until near 11pm when Sam's drug dealer came in and then Paula was right, the atmosphere changed and the drinks over the bar stopped flowing and the drugs took over. When the first punter came up to buy a *Red Bull* Paula looked at me and I looked at him, his jaw was going a mile a minute and he was twitching all over the place. He was out of his tree and had no control so when I asked him for 5 euros for the *Red Bull,* he was happy enough to pay it.

I turned to Paula, "Did you see the state of him?"

"I know Jonny, god knows what he is putting up his nose, he was a real mess."

"I know, this has to stop, someone is going to lose their life taking that shit. I don't want it happening in my bar."

"Well I did warn you, it will get worse before it gets better Jonny and to be honest I don't want to be here when it happens and have the Policia question me about whether I knew drugs were being sold here."

"Paula, trust me, this will be sorted before Harry starts on Friday night."

"You seem really sure about that Jonny, what are you going to do?"

"Never you mind, you just need to know that come Friday there won't be any more drugs sold in our bar."

"What do you mean our bar? I just work here."

"We need to discuss your position here."

"What do you mean Jonny?"

"I want you to buy half the bar Paula."

"Jonny, I wouldn't be in a position to buy half."

"We will work the details out next week but I just need you to know that I want you in as a partner, not just an employee."

"I'm really flattered Jonny but I'm not sure if I'm ready for that."

"We will talk about it next week Paula."

"Ok, thanks for thinking of me like that."

We got on with the rest of the night and it just got worse, the crowd got younger and more out of control. I had to throw a few out for fighting and I even caught a stray punch into the bargain, again it was around 2am when we got the last of them out. When Sam's man was leaving he smiled at me and said, "Takings good tonight Jonny?"

"Just get out," I replied in anger.

"No need to be ignorant," he said, laughing, and walked out

I knew then I would probably have to execute him as well but I would have to see if he would be stupid enough to come back after Sam is dead.

As we locked the bar up, Paula said goodnight and I headed home.

I had the next day off and I spent it with Karen and the kids, we headed down to a place called Quadamar, it was a real wee Spanish town with a beautiful beach that's stretched about 3 miles long. It was stunning and a lovely place to spend the day, we built sandcastles with the kids and went in and out of the sea, we had a lovely lunch together and then headed home around 3pm as it was getting too hot for the kids.

I just lazed about the house for the rest of the day watching a bit of TV and playing with the kids.

The kids went down to bed around 8pm and Karen

and I sat out having a couple of drinks and playing a game of cards. I loved getting the kids to bed and so did Karen, they were getting hard work as they were into everything, crawling around the house pulling absolutely anything down or out onto the floor. It always took about half an hour tidying up after them.

"Karen, why don't you go and get the kids new beds tomorrow as they are getting too big for their cots? If you ask Paula to go with you I will treat you all to lunch in that lovely restaurant in Torrevieja, the one that looks over the ocean?"

"Yeah I would love that, I wanted to have a catch up with her anyway, could maybe see about getting some bed clothes while we are there. I will text her now to see if she is free."

'Super,' I thought, I needed her and the kids off side while I went to work.

We went to bed around 11pm, a bit drunk to be honest, but it was one of the better days.

I woke the next morning, this was the day I finish the job. I couldn't even eat breakfast, I blamed it on feeling a bit hungover but really I was nervous as hell and worried what the day would bring.

I gave the kids a kiss and when I kissed Karen I hugged her just that little bit tighter I didn't want to let go but knew I had to and had to get on with what was in front of me.

On the drive up to Alicante Airport I had time to think, I asked myself if this was the right road to take and go back to killing or should I run away and start up a new life somewhere else with Karen and the kids? As I arrived up at the car park I switched motors and as I sat in the Audi I lifted Mick's file and read through it another time. He had quite a reputation, he was big time and had his hand in absolutely everything, in his file it read that he had supplied explosives to the I.R.A and that's what made me realise that he had to die.

As I drove back down the motorway the car was as smooth as silk, it was lovely to drive. I accelerated faster and looked at the speedo: 60, 70, 80, 90, 100, this thing could shift. When I had it at 120 I took the foot off a bit as I didn't want to get pulled over for speeding, or worse, have an accident but I then knew if I needed a quick getaway this was the thing to do it. I pulled into a bit of waste ground just before the Benidorm turn off and got out to get geared up, I walked round to the back of the motor and opened the boot, I opened up my bag and I lifted out my work clothes which were a pair of khaki trousers a grey t-shirt and a darker grey jacket, I then put on a pair of dark steel toe cap shoes and I was set. I lifted the hidden shelf and picked my weapon of choice, which was the hand gun with the silencer, I placed it in the inner pocket of my grey jacket so it was concealed. I also took a knife which was in a holster, I put it down the back of my trousers and as I took a step back I felt good, I felt ready.

I got back into the car and started it up, as I looked at the clock it read 12.45 so I knew I had about an hour to be in position. I gave a couple of big revs and spun the wheels and I was off, as the car skidded sideward I steered it back straight. Within a few seconds I was back up to 80 mph and as I took the turn off to Benidorm I slowed down, I came into the town and within 10 minutes I was parking the car.

I looked at my watch: 1.05pm, I gripped the steering wheel and took a couple of deep breaths. I was just about to get out when my phone rang, "Operation life's a beach."

"Hello, what's up?"

"Target two not available, just go with target one."

"What do you mean?"

"Target two didn't leave N. Ireland, so one hit only, speak soon," and he hung up.

I didn't know what to think, should I continue or abort? I looked at my watch again: 1.10pm, I was running out of time, I had to make a decision. I banged the steering wheel. "Fuck it, let's do this," I said as I got out and locked the car up. I placed the key in my pocket, felt for my gun and then my knife, I made sure neither of them were visible and I made the short walk round to the café.

My heart was pounding, when I walked around the corner I looked in, in anticipation and there sat in his usual seat was Mick and his minder. His minder looked up at me then glanced down into his newspaper, as for Mick he was shovelling his lunch into his bake, he didn't even come up for a breath. I walked past him and sat inside the café and near the entrance to the toilets.

I ordered a coffee and lifted a paper and tried to just blend into the background. I sat glancing between the paper, Mick and my watch, it read 1.45pm, I knew this was it. I folded the paper and got up from the table, I looked over and Mick was wiping his mouth, I knew I hadn't much time to get set. I walked into the toilet and as I got to one off the cubicles I lifted out of my back pocket a piece of paper which I had written OUT OF ORDER on. I stuck it to the front of the door and went inside and locked the door behind me, I lifted out my gun, checked that it was ready to go and stood up on the toilet and just waited. It was quiet, not a sound, just the beating of my heart. I did my best to slow my breathing down, I crouched down a bit and I felt surprisingly calm. I waited another few minutes which seemed like an eternity and then the main door of the toilet opened and I heard footsteps, I waited, I then noticed a set of shoes just outside my cubicle. I knew this was the minder and he was doing his check before Mick came in, the door moved slightly as he tried to open it and then he walked off. I heard him open the other cubicle door beside me and then he walked out, as he opened the main door I heard him say, "It's clear Mick, you can go in."

I breathed in and out slowly, my heart was thumping, I was shaking a bit. I heard him come in, he went straight into the cubicle beside me, I heard him undo his belt and pull the zip down on his trousers. He sat down on the toilet, he gave a big sigh out, I stood up with my gun in my hand, I was now overlooking the divider that separated the two cubicles. I reached over my right arm with the gun now pointing at Mick, he didn't even look up, I waited for a few seconds. He went into one of his pockets and took out his phone, I watched as he went into his contacts and as he scrolled down he stopped at Sam's number, he pressed the call button so I waited to hear his conversation, I slowly moved my arm back over the divide and listened.

"Hello Sam, do we still have a deal?" I couldn't hear Sam's reply. "I have a boat coming into Ardglass harbour tomorrow night at 10pm, it is a fishing boat, the captain is called Declan, he is your contact. Your gear will be on it but I need the transfer done before you can pick it up." Again, I couldn't hear his reply. "I will text you the account details now so have it done within the hour and the deal is on." Mick paused, Sam was talking to him then Mick said, "Yes, it's all there, explosives and the guns, just make sure the money goes through." He hung the phone up and replaced it in his pocket, I pointed the gun back at him and then as I squeezed the trigger, *thump*, the bullet went right through the top of his head. The blood splattered everywhere and Mick slumped forward and what was left of his head rested against the toilet door. He was dead. I stepped down from the toilet seat and opened the locked door, I reached under the other cubicle and lifted Mick's phone which had fallen out of his pocket. I placed it in my pocket and went to the window, I got up on the unit that was in front of the window, lifted out my knife and with the butt of it I smashed it out with one good shove. The iron bars came loose and fell out, I clambered through the opening and dropped down the 5 foot drop to the waste ground out the back of the café.

As I stood there shaking I bent down and lifted the bars and replaced them in the hole I had just climbed through. I calmly walked off and around the corner to my parked car, I opened it up and got in, I sat in the driver's seat with such a feeling of relief that I had got the job done clean without a messy shoot out with Mick's minder.

I started my car up and drove into the main street of Benidorm and filtered into the busy traffic, as I sat at a set of traffic lights I heard sirens, it was a police car and an ambulance.

I turned my air-conditioning up as I laughed and said, "No point you coming, he is well dead, you would be better with a body bag and a hearse."

The traffic lights turned green and off I headed back to Alicante airport; as I went up the motorway my phone rang, I answered it, exited the next turn off and parked on a hard shoulder.

"Operation life's a beach."

"Operation executed target went cleanly and on my way to level 2," I replied.

"Super, you are booked onto flight 24MZN6 Aer Lingus 18.35pm for Belfast, Operation life's a beach isn't complete yet. Target two's details will be waiting for you in your car which is parked in the long stay car park, row J bay 29, when you arrive."

"Hold on, you mean tonight?"

"Yes, tonight, this has to be finished or it could be detrimental to your family, so be on that flight."

He hung the phone up and I was left there sitting in my car, furious at having to live a double life again and lie to Karen.

I lifted my own phone and rang Karen, "Hello love, how's it going?"

"Yes love, we are sitting here in our favourite restaurant, all our shopping done and we are treating ourselves to a glass of wine and a beautiful lunch. How's your day been?"

"Eventful to say the least."

"That's good, you sound different Jonny, what's up?"

"I am going away for a couple of days, I had forgot all about it until I got a phone call earlier on."

"What do you mean you're going away?"

"It's business, I am going to look at a complete makeover for the bar, but it's up in Valencia so I'm booked in tonight and tomorrow as the meeting is 10.30 in the morning. Then I am meeting a guy tomorrow night at a club to look at his set up and his lighting and sound system, so I am away the next couple of days love."

"You're a geg Jonny, if your head wasn't screwed on you would forget it."

I laughed a forced laugh, I hated lying to her but she bought it.

"I know love, just that much going on at the minute my head is all over the place." I thought to myself, *'Like Mick's head all over the cubicle walls.'* "I will be back probably after lunch on Friday, can you tell Paula to hold the fort and if she needs extra staff in just to go ahead."

"I will do, Jonny is everything ok?"

"Couldn't be better, look I will give you a ring tomorrow after the meeting."

"Ok love, speak to you then."

At that I hung the phone up and was relieved at getting that out of the way.

CHAPTER 19

The Cover Of Darkness

As I arrived at Alicante airport I didn't have much time for the turnaround, I switched the cars but had to go out and do the loop and re-park my Fiesta, lucky enough it was only two spaces down from my Audi so I made it into the airport and got checked in on time.

I sat in the bar in the departure lounge, I got something to eat and I was able to catch my breath. This was really moving fast and I needed time to think, as I sat there I took Mick's phone out, I flicked through it and saw that he was still logged into his bank account. I looked at the balance and it read 84,501, my eyes lit up, I transferred 84,000 of it to my account. I took the back cover off his phone, removed the sim card and threw it into the nearest bin. It was a good day's work. It wasn't long before my flight was called and I boarded the plane.

As I sat waiting for the plane to take off, I went to

turn my personal phone off and saw that I had got a text from Karen, it read, *'I love you Mr Andrews see you soon xx'*

It brought a lump to my throat, how the hell am I doing this again and what if I didn't make it back? I took a deep breath and turned the phone off.

I went to turn the work phone off and it had a text as well, it read, *'Target 1 complete will make contact soon as you land.'*

I held the power button in and turned it off, I just stared at the back of the seat in front of me. I was miles away when the girl sitting beside me said, "Are you nervous about flying?"

"Sorry, I was miles away there, no I'm ok."

"Oh right, I'm Sarah, were you on holiday?"

"No, I live in Spain."

"So what has you going back to Belfast?"

I thought to myself, *'What a nosey bitch.'* "I am there on business."

"I was on holiday with my mates but we didn't pre-book our seats and they are all up the back of the plane."

I looked around and yep, there were her mates and all as drunk as her. They waved down and one of them shouted down, "You're not safe sitting with her mate, she will eat you alive."

I just laughed and turned back again, Sarah put her hand on my leg. "They aren't wrong you know, have you ever heard of the mile high club?"

"I have love and I'm not interested." I lifted her

hand and placed it on her own leg, *'This is all I need,'* I thought, *'some horny girl wanting to have sex with me on a plane.'* I think she got the message when I switched seats and sat by the window, leaving an empty seat between us.

For the rest of the flight she ordered drink after drink and by the time we got to Belfast she could hardly stand, never mind walk off the plane.

As I walked through security and showed my passport I was still unsure about being Scott Fraser, I kept waiting to get pulled in or arrested but it all went smooth. I walked outside of the airport, lifted my work phone out and turned it on, I walked towards the long stay car park and the phone rang. "Operation life's a beach, you're back in Belfast then?"

"Yes I am, where's the keys for the car?"

"Behind the front wheel, driver's side, I will ring you in an hour once you've read your mission."

He hung the phone up and I walked to row J, I was slightly confused, I already knew my mission: SAM. *'What is Drew going on about?'* I thought. I walked down the row and knew straight away which car I was to get, a black Audi, exactly the same as mine in Spain. I bent down, reached behind the front wheel and felt for the keys and yep, there they were. I stood up and opened it up, I placed my bag in the back seat and opened the boot where there was a large grip bag. I looked around to make sure there was nobody about before I opened it. I slowly pulled back the zip, again there was a brown envelope and some clothes, I lifted the envelope out and zipped the bag back up. My inquisitive mind made me lift the shelf which the bag sat on and my eyes lit up, there were 5 guns, 3 knives and what really caught my eye was a machine gun with a silencer attached to it. I was busting to lift it out but couldn't do it here in the middle of the car park so I lowered the shelf and closed the boot, I walked around and got into the car.

As I sat holding the brown envelope it felt good, I was now Scott Fraser, hired killer for MI6. I couldn't wait to get to the Bastard Sam and make him pay for all his wrong doings.

I opened the envelope and poured its contents out onto the passenger seat, it contained a series of photos and a piece of paper, I started reading it,

'Sean McMullan I.R.A sniper credited for 5 killings including 4 police officers, he is currently living in Donegal but has been seen in Bundoran in the Kicking Donkey bar. This is top priority and is to be taken out by Friday as we have information that he has selected his next target and it's to happen on Saturday.'

I sat there numb, I thought I was coming to Belfast to get Sam, why have I to go and kill this guy? I shook my head in disgust, they really had me on the end of a rope, a puppet doing their dirty work. I looked at what else was on the seat beside me: a set of keys and a note, 'Apartment 85 Obel Tower Belfast Lagan side.' There was also a wad of cash and a parking ticket, I flicked through the money and there must have been a couple of grand, all 20 pound notes. I set it back down along with the piece of paper, I lifted the photos and had a look at who I was to kill, it wasn't what I expected. He was an old-ish looking man, he must have been in his late fifties with grey slicked back hair and had a goatee beard. He actually looked very distinguished, but if this was my target he had to die.

I put the keys in the ignition and started the car, I drove up to the security barrier, put my window down and placed the parking ticket into the machine. It surprised me when the ticket came back out again and the barrier lifted, I frowned and just drove out, putting the ticket into the sun visor. I headed for Belfast and to the apartment that I had the keys for.

As I arrived at the apartment I parked the car and went into the building, it was a beautiful big high rise right on the river Lagan. I got into the lift and pressed the button for the 15th floor, the lift was really smooth and within seconds the doors opened and I walked to the apartment.

When I walked in through the front door it took my breath away, it was stunning, all the best furniture. I took a walk round and I said to myself, "I could get used to this." I stood at the window looking out over Belfast, I noticed the speeding traffic go over the M3 and the Odyssey complex just to the right hand side and then the large cranes, Samson and Goliath, in the docks. It really was some view.

My phone started ringing and I knew it was Drew.

"Hello, why am I not here to finish the job?"

"Listen, you need to take this target out, it's important that you execute him, it will save lives."

"I understand that but what about my target?"

"This is priority, it has to be done first, then you can take your target down."

"Do I have a choice?" I said angrily.

"No, you don't, you are employed by me and I need you to be focused."

"I need more time, my target is set for tomorrow night."

"Keep your target time but you need to be in Donegal on Friday morning."

"As long as everything goes well on Thursday night then it's doable, just keep me updated on his movements."

"Will do, good luck, I will speak with you Friday morning."

He hung the phone up and left me with my mind buzzing, Sam would be easy, just pick my moment and nut him but it was the unknowing that worried me. I had never been to Donegal and didn't know who or what I was going to face.

I unpacked my bag and with it being just after 9pm, I was starving. I left the apartment and went to a local chip shop where I sat in and had a battered sausage, super, and a tin of *Coke*, I had forgot how tasty the chippers was and enjoyed every mouthful.

I then returned to the apartment and as I lay on my bed I gave Karen a ring to see if everything was ok back home. I didn't stay on the phone too long as I had a big day ahead of me.

I had a restless night's sleep, tossing and turning most of the night, I think the last time I looked at my watch it was 4.35am so when I got up at 8am I got a shower to try and wake myself up.

I left the apartment and went for breakfast, I decided to drive to Ardglass and case the area out and pick my spot to shoot Sam. I arrived down around 11am and as I parked my car in this sleepy wee port I could see why this is where the pickup was to be, as it was like a ghost town, hardly a sinner about. There were a few good vantage points but it would all depend on where Sam parked his car, the harbour only had one way in and out and he would probably be focused solely on his pickup meaning I had the upper hand. I decided that I would just walk down and using the darkness of the night as my cover, I would kill whoever was there right on the harbour's edge.

I took a drive into Downpatrick just to waste some time and sitting in a side street café I caught up on the local news in the Belfast telegraph. It was just the same old crap, politicians not agreeing on how to run the country, but one piece of news grabbed my attention. The I.R.A were accused of robbing a bank in the middle of Belfast and no, not just the usual balaclavas and guns, they loaded a van in the dead of night and got away with a staggering 26.5 million pound in used notes. *'Only in N. Ireland could this happen,'* I thought, *'but what an amount of money.'*

I flicked to the sports section to see how the mighty Linfield was doing, they were top of the league with 10 games played losing only 1 game to Glenavon, and the front two of Glen Ferguson and Peter 'the postman' Thompson netting 18 goals between them. They looked like they were going to rump the league but it was an upcoming young defender called Jim Ervin that caught my eye. The Shankill Road lad was getting great reviews for his no nonsense defending and he was cementing his place in the team at the age of 19.

I loved hearing about lads from the Shankill doing well, especially at Linfield, the club I worshipped.

When I finished reading, I took a walk around the town but Downpatrick was a one horse town with not much in it so I decided to go for a drive and maybe find a bit of waste ground to get the feel for my machine gun. I hadn't tested it yet and worse, I had never held such a big gun before.

About 2 or 3 miles out in the country I came across a derelict farm building, it was perfect, so I parked the car and got the gun out. As I examined it closer I found the safety, I aimed it at a tree and squeezed the trigger, it was amazing with the silencer attached, it hardly made a sound. It popped bullets out in a rapid manor, it was pure brilliant, the power this gun had and the feeling I had was superb. I practised a few times lowering it and raising it quickly and finding my target for about an hour then went back to the car and reloaded it and got myself changed into my work clothes, which were all black. I couldn't wait to see the look on Sam's face when I put a bullet into him.

I drove back round to Ardglass but stayed outside the town for a while in a secluded laneway, it was now 6.45pm and I knew it would be 3 hours before I needed to be in place so I decided to have a doze for an hour or so. I put the radio on, put my seat back and closed my eyes. I didn't want to over sleep so I set an alarm on my phone.

I swear I had only closed my eyes when the alarm went off and I awoke with a jerk, my heart was racing and it was pitch black outside, you couldn't see 2 feet in front of you. I took a couple of deep breaths, had a drink of water, started the car and headed for the Harbour. As I drove around the twisty roads I kept looking at the time, 9.30pm, just enough time to get parked up and wait for Sam.

I arrived at my parking spot that overlooked the harbour and when I got set I just sat in the car and waited, at 9.50pm I could see a fishing boat pull in to the harbour and moor up. This is it, this is the boat, then a black Range Rover drove by where I was parked. I slouched down in my seat as it passed and I sat and waited another few seconds while it parked right beside the boat. Then there he was, that fat bastard Sam, large as life with two of his usual cronies to protect him, but not tonight, they weren't going to stand a chance against me and my gun. I reached up and made sure the interior lights were switched to off then I got out, I was about 50 yards away, I could see them clearly starting to off load the guns and explosives. I slowly walked towards them using the cover of darkness and crates that were stacked along the way to keep me hidden, 20 yards, 10 yards, I took the safety off my gun. I raised it and came out from behind a stack of wooden boxes, with a puff of air and a flash of my gun, I shot the two minders first. It was like everything moved in slow motion as half their heads were taken off, round after round I fired, killing all in my path. I walked towards the boat, Sam tried to get back into the Range Rover but I shot him in the legs and left him lying, squealing in pain. I moved on to the captain of the boat and his two crew who were shouting, "Don't shoot, don't shoot," with their hands in the air, but they had picked the wrong guy to deal with so *bang, bang, bang* and the three of them lay dead on their boat. I turned and walked to where Sam was now trying to crawl away and as I stood over him he turned onto his back and was looking straight up at me. I pointed my gun at him as he said, "You."

I replied, "Who else, you piece of shit?"

"Fuck you Jonny, your family is dead, my contact in Spain will kill them all."

"I think you will find Mick is dead and as for your payment, I have taken that too."

The look on his face said it all, I think he realised he wouldn't be walking away from this and as I slowly shot him again in the chest he let out a scream. I watched as the blood oozed out of his body and towards the edge of the harbour, watching the life drain from him. He just stared at me, he never spoke, he just gasped for air, then one last breath and he was dead.

As I walked back past the boat I noticed the name on the side of it, 'FREEDOM' it said and I thought to myself, *'You are all free now,'* and gave a smile. I walked back to my car and put my gun back in the hidden compartment of the boot, got in and with great satisfaction I drove away.

CHAPTER 20

Homeward Bound

It took me about 40 minutes to get back to the apartment and when I did I went straight in for a shower. It didn't even fizz on me that I had killed 6 men, my head was all messed up but I enjoyed the power, and knowing that Sam didn't have a hold on me anymore was a huge relief.

As I sat watching the TV my phone rang, "Operation life's a beach."

I had a smug tone to my voice as I answered, "Target down."

"Well done, you not only took out your target but three Polish arms smugglers as well, a super night all round. You really are a great find, we could have a very interesting future working together."

I was grinning from ear to ear. "I'm here to help and will be in place by lunch time tomorrow but after then I need to get home and sort things out back there."

"Absolutely, your payment will be in the account tomorrow, and good luck."

"Thanks." I hung the phone up and rubbed my hands together. "Jonny, you are a piece of work, I think you have found what you are good at, or should I say Scott Fraser."

I went to bed and had a great night's sleep.

In the morning I rang Karen and told her that I would be home hopefully later on that night, she wasn't too well pleased as she thought I was coming home earlier but I spun her another lie that I had another meeting and it would be a late one.

I got myself together and left for Bundoran, as I drove down the motorway I put the satnav on and it gave me an estimated time of 1 hour 40 minutes to my destination, I was totally amazed at this. I had the radio on and as the news came on it gave a brief description of an incident in Ardglass, details were not to be released as there were multiple fatalities and police were keeping an open mind but they were looking into a gang land style feud.

I arrived in Bundoran bang on time and as I drove up the town I noticed the bar, you couldn't miss it as it had a full donkey right above the front doors, so I parked just past it in a side street and headed for the bar.

It was now after 1pm so when I went into the bar I got a table by the window, I could feel a thousand eyes on me and as I looked around the room I caught a few different people staring at me. I just put it down to a strange face in their local bar. When the girl came down to take my order she started asking some questions, "On holiday love?"

"No, I'm here on business."

"Oh right, and what sort of business would that be?"

"The sort that's none of your business, could I just order some lunch please?"

The girls face went a bit red, I didn't know if she was just being friendly or was trying to find out who I was and where was I from but to be honest, I couldn't be arsed with the small talk. I just wanted to case the place and get something to eat.

"Sorry if I seemed rude, I just haven't seen you in here before and with that tan I know you're not local."

"You are right there, I'm not and to be honest, as soon as I get this piece of business over the better, I can't wait to get back on a plane and go home."

"But your accent is from up north?"

"Yeah, I'm originally from Belfast, but I've been living in Spain for a few years now."

"You are so lucky, I would love to live somewhere with better weather than here, all we seem to get is bloody rain. The only difference between summer and winter here is that the rain is warmer in the summer."

I laughed at that, "You are damn right, that's one of the reasons I moved away, could I order the two course special you have on?"

"Yes, what is your starter?"

"Could I have the soup and then for my main could I have the steak and Guinness pie with chips?"

"Good choice, the soup is curried parsnip, it's really nice."

"Sounds lovely."

As the girl left I thought to myself, *'Curried bloody parsnip? This is going to taste well.'*

I sat there just watching out the window and the people walking up and down the street going about their daily routines. It was a busy wee town for the size of it, it reminded me a bit of Newcastle, with the arcades and the shops that sold all the same crap.

5 minutes passed and the girl came over with my soup, she set it down and said, "Enjoy sir, can I get you a drink?"

"Thanks, yeah, could I have a pint of *Coke* please?"

"Certainly, I will bring it over with your main."

As I lifted my spoon and tried the soup, the girl was right, it was really tasty and the whack of wheaten bread I got you could have used as a door stop. I spread a bit of butter across it and took a bite, it was as tasty as the soup, I really enjoyed it and just wished the bowl was bigger. I mopped up the last of the soup with the wheaten bread and shoved it into my mouth.

As my main was set down to me about 10 minutes later my eyes lit up. The pie came out in its own separate dish and the puff pastry sat about 2 inches higher than the dish, the girl commented on how clean my bowl was, "I take it you enjoyed the soup?"

"Aye love I did, you won't need to wash that bowl, I licked it clean."

She laughed as she set my *Coke* down and left.

I emptied the pie onto my plate and the gravy ran under my chips, I got stuck into it and I didn't come up for air, it was gorgeous.

I finished it in about 20 minutes and sat over my *Coke* for another 20 or so; there was no sign of my target and I was getting impatient, I didn't know whether to stay or go. When I asked for my bill my phone rang, "Operation life's a beach, your target is on route, he is in a silver BMW X5 and should be arriving inside 30 minutes so be prepared. This won't be as straight forward as your last."

"No worries, I will meet him soon."

The girl looked at me, "Is your meeting postponed? I couldn't help over hearing."

"Yeah, just a bit, I have to meet him up the road. The lunch was lovely, keep the change."

I really didn't want to get into a whole conversation so I left.

I walked down the street and around the corner where I had parked, I decided to move the car into the main street and sit and wait for him to arrive.

As I sat there I was slowly getting nervous, I watched each car that passed and then there it was, the BMW X5 drove past me. I looked in and there were 2 guys in the front and one in the back, I watched as it parked outside the Kicking Donkey and one of the guys got out and opened the back door. I watched closely as the guy got out and yes, it was Sean, he looked around as he walked to the bar and the other guy followed him in. The BMW drove off, I watched in my rear view mirror as it turned and parked not far behind me, the driver got out and walked across the road to join Sean for lunch.

I knew I only had an hour or so to get a plan together, there was no way it could have been done in the bar as it had too many cameras so it had to be done either as they left or on route. I drove off and out of the town to a secluded road just about a mile out and parked.

I opened my boot and lifted the shelf, I stared at my arsenal and decided to go for the machine gun again as it was my favourite. I made sure it was fully loaded, I also lifted a hand grenade just in case I needed it, I closed the boot and got into the car. As I sat looking at the hand grenade it seemed quite simple to operate, hold the trigger, pull the pin and throw. I set it alongside my gun on the passenger seat and put my coat over them, I then drove back down to the town and parked a few cars back from the BMW and waited.

I patiently watched the bar and my watch, it was like watching paint dry. I was ready to go, I just wanted to get started and then one of the guys came out on his own. He walked over to the motor and got in, my heart was racing, this was it. I threw my coat on the floor and lifted the gun but then the guy in the BMW drove over to other side of the street and Sean and his minder got into the motor and they sped off. I started my car and followed, we headed out of the town, I was about 3 cars back and I could see the BMW speed off and get further away. I was getting frustrated as the further they got it seemed like the cars in front of me got slower, I banged my fist on the steering wheel and said, "Fuck me, get out of my way." The BMW was now out of sight, I got to a straight bit of the road dropped down a gear and floored it, my Audi took off like a bat out of hell and I sped past the 3 cars and in a panic tried to catch up.

Bend after bend I went round at about 60/70 mph and it was only when I got to the carriageway that I spotted the silver BMW. I hadn't a clue what to do, do I just follow or do I ram their motor? But as I got closer there was no chance my car would push theirs off the road, I would just make a mess of my own so I just slowed down and filtered in behind a car and got my thoughts together and waited. I followed for about 10 minutes and then when they turned off and joined the motorway I decided to take them out there, I put my passenger side window down, drove alongside them and lifted my machine gun. I started firing at their car, everything was silent, I could just see the smoke rise from my gun and their car swerving away and crashing into the side barrier that ran alongside the motorway. I slowed down and pulled in behind the crashed car, I quickly lifted my hand grenade and with my gun I got out of my car. As I walked, focused on their car, I hadn't even noticed the other cars that had got caught up in this; I walked slowly closer to their car, one of the doors flung open and a staggering figure emerged, I shot him straight away and he fell to the ground. I then approached the motor, I pointed my gun inside, the other two were knocked out and weren't moving. I shot the other minder straight away and as I looked at Sean, he was starting to come around. I said to him, "Sean McMullan?"

He lifted his blooded face and spat blood at me and said, "This won't end here you Brit."

I put one in his head and one in his chest and as he slumped back into his seat I turned and walked back to my car. I looked around, there were 3 other cars crashed but car after car was driving past and blasting their horns, I knew then it was time for me to get out of there. I lowered my gun and ran to my car, as I got in I threw my gun in the passenger seat and sped off, I had to swerve to miss another crashed car but I got away clean. I floored the accelerator and had the car up to 100mph in a few seconds, I kept at this speed for a few minutes and then slowed down and headed for Belfast. I had only got about 10 miles away when I noticed in my rear view mirror the flashing lights of a police car, my heart started pounding and I sped up 70/80/90 mph, but it got closer. I knew they were after me so I gripped the steering wheel and said, "So let's see how fast you can go." I floored it and the car shot forward, as it got faster and faster I looked at the speedo: 140mph, this thing could shift. I looked in my rear view mirror and the police car was getting further and further away, I was hammering down the motorway and I kept at this speed for a few miles. I came up to slip road, braked quickly and turned off, I travelled along this road for a few miles and then pulled over.

I was shaking like a leaf and breathing very erratically, I thought to myself, 'That was too close, I was lucky to be driving such a fast car,' and then I got to thinking that I would have to dump the motor and make my way back to Belfast a different way.

So I drove up the road a bit and took the turn off

for Enniskillen, about 10 minutes up the road I saw a sign that said 8 miles to Enniskillen. I past it and there was another sign that said Lough Navar forest park so I pulled in and drove in. I spotted a laneway on the right-hand side so I drove up it, it was nearly overgrown the further I drove up it. I stopped and got out, I opened the boot and took out what I needed and then closed the boot again. I stood wondering what to do to make sure I wouldn't be connected to it, it was extreme but I decided to open the boot again and as I stood about 10 feet away, I lifted the hand grenade. I squeezed the trigger, removed the pin and as I held my breath I lobbed it into the boot. I turned, took to my heels and sprinted back down the lane, as I got about a hundred yards away it went off and what a bang it went. I fell to the ground and as I lay there, bits of the car fell around me, they were right big chunks of motor. I got up and turned to look towards the now blazing car and as I stood there I heard bullets going off, one whizzed past my ear and that was my cue to get off side. I ran the other 100 yards or so back to the main road and headed for Enniskillen.

CHAPTER 21

Sleeper

I walked for about 10 minutes then the rain came on and it was quite heavy; I zipped my coat up and raised the collar but it didn't really stop the soaking I was getting. Car after car passed me as I looked up the road and spotted a bus stop in the distance so I started walking that little bit quicker, wanting to get out of here and back to Belfast.

As I stood at the bus stop I looked at the time table to see what time the next bus was due, I looked at my watch and I had about 25 minutes to wait so I sat on the narrow seat that ran the length of the shelter and lifted my phone out of my bag. I turned it on and rang Karen, "Hi Love, how's you?"

"Jonny, where are you?"

"I'm still up in Valencia but should be heading home later on tonight."

"I have tried ringing you but your phone was off, I was getting really worried."

"It ran out of charge and I had forgotten my

charger so I had to buy another one."

"Oh right, is everything ok?"

"Yes love, just getting things finished off here, I have a surprise for you as well."

"And what's that?"

"Now it wouldn't be a surprise if I told you."

"I hate surprises, just tell me?"

"Absolutely no chance, you will see when I get home, how's the kids?"

"They are fine, missing their daddy though."

"I'm missing them too," I replied with a heavy heart. "I will be home soon."

"Ok, see you then, love you."

"Love you too, see you later."

I hung the phone up and turned the work phone on, I looked at my watch and I had still bloody 10 minutes to wait. The rain was sideways and even though I was under the cover of the bus shelter I was still getting wet, I sat with my head down just staring at the phone willing it to ring. I needed picking up and out of the area but the more I stared, the realization of it not going to ring was more apparent. I knew I was on my own with the exit, as Drew wouldn't have known what went down yet.

I waited and waited and of course the bus was late, but I was glad to get on and out of this crappy weather.

I sat at the window and just stared at the country side as the bus made its way to Enniskillen. It pulled into the bus station, I had to wait on another bus to get to Belfast, I thought it would be a better idea traveling by bus and remain unnoticed. I knew once the peelers got on the scene they would be stopping cars and searching them. The bus was a good cover. I went into the wee shop at the station and bought a couple of bags of crisps, a tin of *Coke* and a bar of chocolate. As I waited on the bus to Belfast I opened up the first packet which was an old favourite *Tayto* cheese and onion, I hadn't had a packet of these in absolute ages and they tasted like I remembered. I washed them down with the tin of *Coke,* gave a big burp and finished the crisps, it wasn't too long of a wait and before I knew it I was on the road again and heading for Belfast.

For the time I spent on that bus I had went round and round in my head at how the hell I was now a killer again and it tormented me. I never wanted to be this man I now was, but to be honest I never had a choice, it just seemed I was destined to become this person. Was it all I was going to be?

I had a bit of a doze to waste some time, and I needed it. The bus pulled into the depot in Belfast and my phone rang, I quickly got off the bus and answered it.

"Where are you?"

"I have just got off the bus in Belfast, I'm walking back to the apartment, I take it you have heard the news?"

"Fuck sake Scott, it's a mess, we need to get you out of the country and quick. You are booked onto a flight at Belfast city for 21.15, can you make it?"

I looked at my watch seeing that it was 6:55. "I need to get changed so it will be tight."

"Just make the flight, we have had information that the I.R.A has a description of you and know you are in Belfast."

The more Drew spoke on the phone the more I listened closely and then it hit me, no code word, this wasn't Drew. A shiver ran down my spine, I was being set up, as I walked over the Queens bridge I didn't know what to do. I just stopped and leant up against the rail and listened on, "Are you near the apartment yet?" I paused. "Scott, can you hear me? Are you at the apartment?"

"Yes I am, I'm just going through the front doors now."

I crossed over and as I stood on the bridge looking over at the apartment blocks' front door I saw a speeding car drive up and screech to a stop. Two masked men got out with guns and ran into the building, I listened and watched as they came back out after a couple of minutes. They looked around the side of the building and then got back into the car, I dropped the phone over the side and watched it as it made a splash and sank into the murky deep water. Again, I didn't know who I could trust but I knew I wasn't safe here.

I hastily walked into the city centre and headed for the taxi rank, as I walked towards it my own phone rang, it was a withheld number so I wasn't sure whether to answer it or not. I stood looking at it and as it rang and rang I decided to answer it, but I didn't speak.

"Operation life's a beach, mission compromised, exit lower north street, be there in 5," and he hung up. I had no other choice, I headed for the meeting point and just prayed it was legit, as I walked up lower north street a van pulled up alongside me and the side door was flung open. I turned to face it and Drew got out, "Jonny get in, come on, we haven't much time."

I followed him back into the van and as I sat down he got in beside me and slammed the door. He shouted, "Go, go, go." The van sped off and as it travelled up the road at speed Drew asked me, "Are you ok?"

"I'm fine, what happened?"

"Someone leaked your information, you're lucky to get out."

"Who?"

"We have a mole in the unit and that's how we lost our last agent, Jonny your family is in danger, we need to get them out."

"What is a mole?"

Drew looked at me really worried, "Jonny, a mole is a double agent, they are feeding the I.R.A your movements and will stop at nothing to get to you."

"Fuck I need to get home, I need to phone Karen."

I lifted my phone but Drew stopped me, "Wait Jonny, compose yourself."

"I don't care, I need to get Karen and the kids out of there."

"Is she home now?"

"I think so." I looked at my watch, it was now 20

past seven so it was 20 past eight back home. "She will be in the middle of putting the kids to bed."

"Ring her but be calm Jonny, if she thinks they are in danger then she will panic, is there anyone else you can get to pick them up and take them somewhere safe?"

I thought for a second who could I trust enough, it had to be Paula.

"Paula could get them, but where could she take them?"

"You have a flat above the bar, don't you?"

"Yes I do Drew."

"Then take them there, it's a public place so they wouldn't try anything."

I dialled Paula's number, she answered straight away, "Hi Jonny."

"Paula listen to me, I need a favour."

"Anything, what do you need?"

"I need you to go straight to my house and pick Karen and the kids up and take them to your flat."

"Jonny you sound worried, what's wrong?"

"I can't go into it but just promise me you will go now?"

"I will, I'm leaving straight away."

"Thanks Paula, I will be home soon."

I hung the phone up and held it tightly in my hands. "I fucking knew this would go tits up, this is all your doing Drew." I looked angrily at him.

"Calm down Jonny, we will get your family safe and then we need to find out who this mole is."

"And how the hell are you going to find that out?"

"We will get you back to Spain then it's a case of feeding certain information to certain people, then we will know who it is."

"I don't understand Drew, does that not mean I will be in the firing line?"

"Not necessarily, but you will have to be involved."

I hadn't a clue what he meant and I was getting agitated, I just wanted to get home to make sure Karen and the kids were safe.

"Where are we going now?"

"To get you on a flight and out of Northern Ireland."

As we drove up the motorway I looked up at one of the signs, it read International airport. I knew it wasn't too far and I just sat silent and in my own thoughts, as did Drew.

After about 20 minutes I was outside the main entrance, we both got out of the van and as I stood there I asked, "So what happens now?"

"Just go back home Jonny, I will be in touch."

"That's no good to me, it won't be safe." I was really annoyed. "Just go home, just go fucking home?"

"Jonny calm down, you're causing a scene."

"Causing a fucking scene? That's the least of my worries."

"Look Jonny we will get this sorted on our end, you are a skilful operative and I am certain that you can handle anything your end. We want you to keep a low profile and I will contact you when I find out who is working against us."

"So is that it, am I out?"

"No Jonny, you're what we call in the business as a sleeper, I will be in touch."

Drew turned and got back into the waiting van and it drove off, I stood and watched it make the turn back onto the Belfast road. I walked into the airport and checked in, as I got through security and sat on one of the many seats I gave a sigh of relief and just thought how different this could have turned out.

CHAPTER 22

Hardman Harry

I didn't make it back home until the early hours but when I walked through the door to the flat Karen and Paula were waiting for me.

"Jonny, what is going on, why do we have to stay here?" Karen asked.

"Take a walk with me and I will explain, Paula will you stay and mind the kids?"

"Yes, no problem," Paula replied also really worried looking.

We left the apartment and walked towards the beach, as we walked along the water's edge we held hands, I could tell she was worried and rightly so.

"Sam has put a hit out on me and I was worried that he would come for you and the kids."

"What do you mean, kill you?"

"Yes love, at any cost."

She threw her arms around me. "Jonny, what are we going to do?" she asked through her tears.

I absolutely hated lying to her but it was the only explanation I could think of, "It was Porter who told me but he also said that he is dealing with it and that we should be more security conscious from now on, I just panicked when I heard." I couldn't have told her the truth, that it is the I.R.A that has a hit out on me, I just hoped that Spain was beyond their reach, but I had to put things in place to keep us all safe. "Porter told me Sam is mixed up with some serious people and that it looks like it's going to go tits up for him, we can only hope he gets killed himself and then it's over."

"Jonny, I have never wished anybody dead but this time I just hope you are right and Sam gets killed."

We stood on Benidorm beach and just hugged and kissed under the moon lit sky, it was lovely, I was glad to be home. We walked back to the apartment and went to bed, I was absolutely shattered but could only manage a few hours' sleep. I was woken up by a loud bang from outside, I jumped out of bed to look out the window and it was the bin men emptying the bar's large bin, as the bottles crashed into the back of the lorry Karen woke up as well.

"We need to go home Jonny, there isn't enough space here and Paula needs her place back."

"Yeah love, we will head home this morning after breakfast when I've sorted the bar out."

The kids woke not long after that. Karen, Paula and myself already had breakfast before the kids got theirs so I was able to open the bar up and get it set up for the day ahead. With it being Saturday it was going to be busy so when we left to head home I told Paula I would do the late shift and be back for 4pm. She was pleased I was back and things were getting back to normal, but normal it wasn't, there was still the matter of Sam's drug dealer and also his 1000 euro to be picked up from the guy on the motorbike.

As we left the apartment and walked around the corner Karen asked, "Jonny, where's the car?"

"That's your surprise love." As I stood beside my gleaming black Audi I said, "Here is our new motor."

"Oh my god Jonny it is gorgeous, this is our motor?" She was really excited as she opened the passenger door. "Jonny, where are the car seats?" *'Shit, I've forgotten to put them in, think quick,'* I thought. "Sure, the kids have outgrown them ones, we will go now and buy two new ones."

"Ok, I will sit in the back with the kids." I started the car and Karen said, "This is beautiful Jonny but can we afford it?"

If only she knew how much money I was sitting on she would never even ask that, "The bar is doing really well and we deserve it love so don't worry, I wouldn't have bought it unless we could."

As we drove up the road and to an outlet store to get a couple of car seats I looked in my rear-view mirror and Karen was smiling from ear to ear.

We got the kids strapped into their seats and, not one of my best ideas, I gave them a bar of chocolate each to eat on the way up home. By the time we got to our house the bloody chocolate was everywhere and the two of them were plastered. I swear when we lifted them both out we walked up the garden path holding them at arm's length. We both laughed at the state of them and just plunked them into their high chairs to get them cleaned up.

After we got our two holy terrors cleaned up we had a bit of lunch and I gave them a kiss and headed back to the bar for my shift and to sort out the two problems that still remained.

On the way down I rang Harry and asked him if he got on ok last night with his first night, he told me about the guy that was selling the drugs and that there was another fella in looking for me. I told him I would meet with him later around seven to let him know why they were there.

I arrived down at the bar around 3.30pm and had a coffee before I started at 4pm, it was quite quiet for the time of year so I was able to get caught up with some paperwork. As I sat in the office, both Peter and Paula came in, "Jonny, can we have a word please?" Peter asked.

I looked up. "This sounds serious, what's up?"

They both sat down in front of me, "We need to know what's going on with the bar Jonny, we don't like drugs being sold on the premises, we also see a guy coming in once a week and you paying him off."

"I'm glad you are both here, look it's like this, the drugs will be stopped tonight I assure you. He won't be back after I have a word, and for the guy that comes in for the money I think you will find he won't be back either."

"But how can you be so sure Jonny?" Paula asked.

"I have friends that have made commitments to

me and I am telling you, we are taking our bar back."

"Look Jonny, it was great at the start but things have changed and I am not sure if I want to keep working for you," Peter replied.

"That's why I don't want you working for me."

"I don't understand, do you want me to leave?"

"No Peter, quite the opposite, I would like you and Paula to become partners then you both will have an equal say on how to improve things and how we can make Buffaloes the best bar in Benidorm."

"I am flattered Jonny, but how would that work?"

"Well first off, we need to buy the lease from Carlos and that's where you both come in. I think we could put an offer on the table he couldn't refuse."

"I don't know if I have the money to do that."

"Look, I want to take a step back from the running of the bar, maybe just pop in now and again. I would put the money up to buy Carlos out but then I would take 40 percent of the profits and you both would get 30 percent each, we would get a contract drawn up so it's all legal and would take away any doubts you both would have."

"That sounds like a dream come true, but do we have to make a decision straight away?"

"Look, what about we meet on Wednesday again, give yourselves a couple of days to think about it?"

"Ok Jonny, that's a good idea."

Paula and Peter thanked me and left, I knew I had to take a back seat from the bar because if there was going to be an attempt on my life it would be here some night after locking up.

When I finished off the paper work I went back out to the bar and got something to eat. I had an appetite like a horse so I had 3 courses and a nice refreshing pint, as I sat eating the bar started filling up. Peter really was a good chef and was giving the bar a great reputation for good food and entertainment.

It was around 6ish when I got behind the bar and started serving and when Harry came in at 7pm I asked to speak with him in the office.

"Sit down mate, I think we need to talk through a few things."

"Yeah, no worries Jonny, I just need to know exactly what my role is here?"

"Look Harry, we have two problems that we need sorted, first there is the man that comes in every night to sell his drugs…"

"I will stop you there Jonny, I am in this game long enough to know he isn't freelancing, he is working for someone that obviously has a hold on you and that is the problem."

I didn't know why but I needed to be honest with him, I had a feeling that I needed him to be closer to me and know who I really was.

"Look Harry, the man you see in front of you isn't who I really am, I have a previous life that has come back to haunt me, but I have removed the threat from the bar, the man that had a grip on me is dead."

I watched him as he took in what I had just told him and then he said, "So what you are telling me is that you killed him or had him killed?"

"Look Harry, I don't know if I can trust you but what I need from you is for you to be my bodyguard, at a distance. I don't want the Mrs or anyone else to know, it might involve getting your hands dirty at times."

"Look Jonny I will be up front with you, I have had a previous life back in Manchester and it was a life I had to leave behind, I was up to my eyes in illegal dealings to say the least. I was second in command of a gang, and don't laugh when I tell you the name of it, this gang was deadly and when I say deadly, we ran Salford. We were called 'THE A TEAM'."

"I had a feeling about you Harry, put it like this, I think we could definitely work closer together. I really need someone with your set of skills."

"It would cost you Jonny."

"How much would you need?"

"2 grand a week."

"That's doable, so we are good to go, we start tonight by taking out the trash."

"It will be a pleasure," Harry replied, he shook my hand and he also had a smile on his face. I think he was missing his previous life and he actually looked excited to get back to being an enforcer again. Harry took his coat off and hung it up in the corner of the room, as he turned to leave he said, "Good to be working with you, boss."

I liked the sound of that, it sounded menacing and with this being the first time I really had met Harry I knew then that I made the right decision. He was a monster of a man, he was wearing a pair of tight blue jeans with an extremely tight white muscle top and what muscles he had, he was huge, he couldn't have put his arms down by his side. His biceps were probably the size of my legs, he had full sleeve tattoos which made him look even bigger, his head was totally shaven with a tattoo on the back of his neck, it was just a series of numbers and I wondered what they meant but that was his business. I was just glad he was working for me and not against me.

"No worries Harry, I will speak with you later when the two problems raise their heads."

At that he left the room, I wasn't too far behind him as I needed to help out behind the bar.

After the food stopped at 9pm I was clearing the tables to make room for a dance floor. I was just about to lift the last table out to the store room when I felt a hand on my shoulder, I turned to see Sam's man standing there holding his motorbike helmet under his arm and his hand out he said to me. "Payment please?" I just stood and stared at him for a few seconds, again he repeated, "Payment, dickhead." I didn't even get to answer him, Harry had him in a head lock and through the front doors before I could even blink. I quickly followed behind him and as I got through the front doors I could just see the back of Harry go around the corner, again I followed and when I turned the corner Harry was beating the guy with his motor bike helmet. He absolutely gave this guy a good going over and he laid in a heap in the alleyway. As I walked up to them Harry stopped beating him, he turned to me and said, "I don't think he will be back boss."

Harry walked back to the around to the bar and as I stood over this guy he was coming around, he sat up at first and as I watched him he tried to get to his feet but just fell to the ground again. I leant down and helped him up and propped him against the wall, he started wiping the blood from his mouth and through his now swelling eyes he said to me, "Sam won't stand for this, you are a dead man."

"I think you will find you are on your own son, Sam is dead."

"What do you mean, how do you know?"

I leant in and said softly, "Because I was the one that put the bullets into him, and if you know what's good for you, you will disappear or I will make you disappear. Do you understand me?"

As he leant up against the wall he was shaking like a leaf, he lifted his head and said, "I will disappear, trust me, I won't be back."

"I don't trust anyone, it's just business and you make it your business never to show your face in Benidorm again 'cause if I ever see you again, the last thing you will see is me pulling the trigger and you felling the burning of a hot bullet as it enters your head. Do you understand me?"

"Yes, yes I do, can I leave now?"

"Not before you empty your pockets."

He started going through each pocket and emptying the contents into his bag that I was now holding open.

"Is that it, can I go?"

"Yes, you can leave," I said as he walked over a

bit, lifted his helmet and then staggered over to the road side where his motorbike was parked. He sort of struggled to put his helmet on and start the bike but once he got it going, he drove off and disappeared up the road.

I returned to the bar walking past Harry on the door, he said to me, "One down Boss, just let me deal with the next ball bag when he comes in."

"No worries Harry, he is all yours."

At 9.40pm the entertainment came in, it was a Robbie Williams tribute act, I had seen this guy before in one of the other clubs and knew I had to get him booked in at least one Saturday night a month. His name was Matt and he was from London, when he walked in he sort of looked a bit like the real Robbie but when he came on at 10pm he was the absolute button of Robbie and the set he did was superb. The place was rocking and absolutely crammed, it was a really busy night. When I looked at my watch at 10.55pm I knew who would be coming in and sure as fate, at 11pm when Matt finished his set and the DJ came on, in he walked. Harry was behind him and as he made his for his usual spot by the toilets Harry looked over at me, I nodded and Harry knew what to do. I ushered Matt into the office to get him paid and out of the corner of my eye I saw Harry trail the man out into the store.

I closed the office door behind me and said, "Matt, you where superb, you are definitely one of my favourite acts doing the circuit."

"You are too kind Jonny, I'm just glad you enjoy it."

As I counted out his 200 euro I asked him, "Where are you next mate?"

"I'm heading to a cruise ship in the morning to play so I will be away for the next month."

"That's brilliant, I'm sure you are looking forward to that, it will be something different than the clubs."

"Aye it will be, it's not as good money as doing the circuit but it's a really nice boat so I'm looking forward to a bit of down time as well."

"I'm sure you are, when are you back in Benidorm?"

"I won't be back until May, after the cruise ship I am in Germany for 3 weeks, there is a massive gig there I do every year. Would you like to fly out and meet me for a few days? We could go on the lash."

"My wife would love me if I disappeared to Germany mate… but I will keep it in mind."

I gave him his money and we said our goodbyes, I had him booked in again when he returned in May.

When I walked back out to the bar, Harry was standing. I looked at him hard and he just smiled, I didn't even ask him what happened I just smiled and nodded back. I returned back behind the bar and started serving drinks, as I stood there Harry was standing over by the front door, I noticed people's reactions, or should I say lack of reactions as they passed him. He really was a Hard ticket and one not to mess with.

CHAPTER 23

Smiles And Laughter

The next few days I was cautious as I had to watch over my shoulder every time I saw a couple of hard looking guys come into the bar. I wondered if this was it and if they were here for me but I suppose it was my fear of getting killed that kept me sharp and always alert. When driving home late at night, I was paranoid that there was someone following me, I got into the routine of always checking under my car before I got into it because during another phone call with Drew he gave me tips on how to look for a device that could be easily attached to the underneath of my motor and that is a favourite way the I.R.A takes out their targets. He also gave me information on the suspected mole and to my surprise it was his personal secretary, she was connected to the I.R.A and had went underground. He told me that I should keep an eye out for her as from the information he gave me, she was suspected to be in Europe somewhere.

After a couple of weeks I started to relax a bit, maybe it was that Christmas was coming up and we were kept busy organising toys for the kids. I racked my brain trying to think of something nice to get Karen.

It was on the Sunday just before Christmas that I organised a Christmas dinner for all the staff and their families in the bar, I had brought in outside caterers so that Peter didn't get lumbered with the cooking but god love him, once a chef always a chef, he couldn't help himself but be in and out of the kitchen to oversee things. Even when his wife gave him an ear bashing he still couldn't stay away.

I had hired this guy called Eddie Kealty, he was a magician/comedian and I was told for a family show he was brilliant.

As we all tucked into our dinner Eddie turned up, he was wearing a full tuxedo with a bright pink dickie bow. As he walked by us he said, "Hope that tastes as good as it smells."

I replied, "Hi Eddie, I am Jonny, would you like some dinner?"

"Well since you are offering, I could murder a pint."

Everyone laughed, I just frowned and thought to myself, 'Jesus, I have found a right one here.'

"Just help yourself behind the bar," I said.

"The last time someone said that to me Jonny I took the till." Again, everyone burst out laughing and even the kids started laughing which made everyone laugh even more, I knew we were in for a good night.

"I'm only joking Jonny." I gave a bit of a smile but

Eddie then said, "But I wasn't joking about the pint."

As he started setting up his gear on stage I went and poured him one and with it being a new barrel, it had quite a head on it. As I gave it to him he said, "Have you got a flake and sprinkles Jonny?"

He really was a funny guy and I just laughed as he took a big gulp and ended up with a beer moustache.

After we finished our meal all the kids sat at the front of the stage to watch his show, he wasn't much of a magician but the tricks he did made the kids wide eyed, they were fascinated with what he was showing them. It was when he made a lovely white dove disappear that even got me amazed, when it somehow appeared on the top of his head he asked the kids, "Have you seen my bird?"

They all point above his head and shouted, "THERE."

He turned around and asked, "Where? It's not here."

Again, the kids shouted even louder, "THERE, THERE IT IS."

And again he said, "You are winding me up, who has taken my bird?"

As he turned the bird shit down the back of his head and neck and all the kids laughed really hard, even the adults went into ruptures, it was hilarious.

He then did a show for the adults, it was called Mr and Mrs and at times I cringed at some of the answers that our friends gave. Next, it was Harry and his girlfriend, she was a bit of a looker, she was into her fitness as much as Harry, she was quite muscly with a spray tan, long blonde hair and it was very obvious she had had a boob job. It was there that Eddie concentrated his questions and with the answers that she gave even I blushed a bit, but it didn't seem to annoy Harry, he just went with the flow and laughed it off.

After Eddie's show we had a disco for the kids and all the adults sat around a couple of tables and enjoyed a few drinks.

At 9pm we called it a night, the kids were getting tired and to be honest, I'd had a bit too much to drink so when Karen suggested us heading on home I was happy to go. We got the kids, said our goodbyes and I asked Peter to lock up after they finished. As I put Josh in his car seat, I on purpose dropped his dummy under the car, I made a bit of a scene about it, but was able to get on my knees and look under the car for a device. I finally reached for his dummy, Karen said, "Did you get it Jonny? Don't worry if you can't, I have a spare one here."

"Yes love, I've got it."

I stood up, sucked the dummy and put it into Josh's mouth, she said, "For frig sake Jonny, you don't know what was on the ground, you're gonna get the mange."

"Five second rule love."

Karen laughed as I did and I got into the passenger seat and we drove home.

By the time we got home me and the kids were fast asleep, Karen gave me a nudge and said, "Right you, you awl drunkard, let's get these kids to bed."

We lifted them out of their car seats and carried them to bed, we sat for a while and had a cup of tea and chatted about Eddie and his show. It was a really good day out and we were now on the countdown to Christmas, which was only 6 days away.

The next day I had a stinker of a hangover, it was lucky I had the next couple of days off and wasn't due back to work until the day before Christmas Eve. I was closing the bar over the Christmas period to give everyone a well-deserved break so it was a lazy day on the sofa for me, but I swear the kids must have known because they tortured the life out of me. Every time I closed my eyes one of them either hit me a slap in the face or climbed up on top of me. Karen thought this was really funny and by lunch time I had had enough and decided to take them out to a local park.

As I strapped the kids into their car seats I asked Karen to go back into the house to get my wallet which gave me time to check the car. Every time I did this I half expected to see a bomb, I was still very worried about the mole that had set me up before and I knew that maybe not today, but someday, I would have to deal with an attempt from the I.R.A on my life, which got me thinking.

As we drove to my favourite town Quadamar we parked beside the local park and took the kids on a walk, with it being December it was quite cold. We walked around the park and came towards the pond, the ducks and other birds were glad of the bread we had brought, we also brought some fruit as well to feed the many turtles that lived in the ponds and it was amazing to see the kids' reactions as they chumped on the fruit. Josh got himself that worked up at one stage, I think he was eating more bread and fruit than feeding the animals. He also tried to climb the fence to grab one and he wasn't too well pleased when I told him off. As for Erin she was really easy going and loved the ducks, she had a hardy wee laugh when the ducks gobbled up the bread, it startled her but it didn't stop her throwing more bread.

As we walked along one of the many streets we called into a nice wee café and had lunch, it was really relaxing and the kids were super. After about an hour or so we headed back home.

I left Karen and the kids in the house and made the excuse that I was going for a run to clear my head, but really I needed to contact Drew about moving house and getting somewhere that had a garage so I could get my car off the street and be more secure and not as much as an easy target.

The phone call didn't go too well as they were struggling to find out where Brenda the mole had went and Drew told me to be on high alert as they have had information that an attempt on my life was going to happen in four to five days, it would be a team of four and one of them was going to be Brenda. He told me that they have a safe house 40 miles away and that I should spend Christmas there and get my family out as soon as possible, by his tone I knew this was going to happen so there really was only one thing to do, get Karen and the kids out. I was going to get them somewhere further away than where Drew said though and then deal with Brenda and her team.

I made a few phone calls and decided that I had to

get Karen home to her mum and dad's and that we would spend Christmas with them, so I booked us flights and we were due to head back to Belfast the following morning.

When I told Karen, I spun her a yarn about it being the kids' first Christmas and that they should be with their nanny and granddad. She was over the moon to go home and see her mum and dad, she wasn't well pleased when I told her I couldn't get home until the bar closed on Christmas eve though, but she understood and to be honest this needed finishing. I couldn't do it knowing that the I.R.A would gladly kill my family as well.

Karen phoned her mum to tell her the news and she was over the moon, so later on that evening when we got the kids to bed we packed a couple of bags and got everything we needed to take back home.

As we sat on our sofa Karen said to me, "Is everything ok Jonny, you don't seem yourself?"

"Everything is fine love, just a bit of a sore head still."

"No Jonny, I know you better than you know yourself, is there something annoying you?"

"No love, I would rather be traveling with you and the kids but I need to be here to sort a few things out."

"Then just come with us, let Paula and Peter sort the bar out."

"If it was only that easy, I would love to but I need to stay."

I think Karen knew there was something else

going on, I could tell by the look on her face. "Jonny, be honest with me, is there someone else?"

"What do you mean, do you think I'm having an affair?" I was in shock at the thought of Karen thinking I was cheating on her.

"You just don't seem yourself, you are very impulsive and we just haven't been as close lately."

I looked at her and she had a tear in her eye, she lowered her head, I moved over closer to her and held her hand. "You are my world, I would never ever cheat on you, I fell in love with you the first time I set eyes on you in the surgery back on the Shankill and I knew then I would spend the rest of my life with you. I love you Karen and always will."

She lifted her head and threw her arms round me and through her tears she said, "I love you too Jonny."

That night we made love and it seemed different, we fell asleep in each other's arms and when we woke the next morning we were still in the same spot. As the sun streamed through the gap in the blinds we just lay for a while cuddling, but it was the sound of the kids in the next bedroom that was our cue to get up.

We had breakfast and then, as the flight was for 12.15, we packed the bags in the car but not before I did my checks. I then went back into the house and lifted Erin, Karen got Josh and we put them into their car seats. It was a funny sort of a drive down to the airport, Karen didn't speak much, she was really quiet. I asked her a couple of times if she was ok and she just smiled and said she was.

When we arrived at the airport I lifted the double buggy out of the boot and put the kids in, Josh fought me the whole way. He really was getting a handful, I got him strapped in and he wasn't happy at all, he squealed the place down, but I stuck his dummy in and he settled down a bit. Erin was a wee angel, she loved getting into the pram, she loved playing with her toy bar that was strapped across it.

Karen pushed the pram and I lifted the bags, it seemed a really long walk to the airport from the carpark. When we checked in and got the bags away, we walked up to the security check point and it was then as I kissed Karen and the kids goodbye it hit me that I might not see them again. I fought the tears back and stood and watched as Karen and the kids walked through and into the duty free shop, she turned back and waved and as a tear travelled down my cheek I took a deep breath and waved back. It was heart breaking but I knew I had to do this, I wasn't worried about me but if anything ever happened to Karen and the kids, that would kill me.

As I drove home I knew I wouldn't be able to deal with this on my own so I phoned Harry and asked him to meet me.

CHAPTER 24

High Speed

I asked Harry to meet me at my house and as we sat talking I asked him 3 questions, "You know I told you about my previous life and why I came to Spain, Harry?"

"I do Jonny, you look worried, what's up boss?"

"I have been told that the I.R.A is going to make an attempt on my life sometime this week."

"Fuck, what are you going to do?"

"Look Harry, it's a two man job, I just need to know, have you ever killed anyone before?"

Harry sat in silence for a few seconds and then he said, "Look Jonny, I was heavily involved in a movement called the B.N.P and to answer your question, I have had my hands dirty a few times."

"So if a situation arrived could you pull the trigger and kill again?"

"How sure are you that this is the I.R.A coming for you?" Harry's mood changed like a switch was turned on, he looked really interested on what I was going to say next.

"It's the I.R.A alright, look, I am an agent for MI6, a hit man if you want to put a label on it but they have the upper hand on this one. My contact assures me that this information is fact and that they already have their team in place and they are not going to stop until I'm dead."

"I bloody knew it, I knew you were more than you let on, have you got equipment?"

"If you mean weapons then yes, I do, I just need you to cover my back when this goes down."

"Oh I will take great pleasure in killing these I.R.A bastards, what's the plan boss?"

I took out my phone and went onto the messages, I opened up a photo that Drew had sent me and it was of Brenda, I showed it to Harry. "This is the target, she will be accompanied by three men, we have no idea of their appearance but whoever is with her are our targets."

Harry took the phone off me, he looked hard at it and then he said, "She was in the bar today boss, but she was alone."

"What?! Are you sure it was her?"

"She is a looker Jonny, it was her long curly ginger hair that caught my eye, she asked for you by name but I told her you wouldn't be in until Friday."

"Then Friday it is, one last thing Harry, now you are on board with me I need to know, can I trust you?"

Harry paused and then said, "Yes boss, you can trust me, we are on the same side."

"Then this is going to happen, we will need to put our heads together and try and work out where they will hit us."

"Do you think they will have a go in the bar?" Harry asked.

"I really don't know, if it was me that would be too dangerous, there would be no escape if it becomes a shootout. I would probably do it when I was in my car, then it could be secure and if they had a fast car it would be an easy get away."

"Then we will expect them to do it when you arrive Friday morning, right outside the bar."

"I think you're right, that's how I would do it. We will do a dry run and get it set up. Now, come with me, I want you to see something."

We both stood up and I walked out of the house with Harry following me. I walked to the back of my car and opened the boot, I lifted my keys and unlocked the hidden shelf. As I opened it Harry's eyes lit up, "Holy shit boss, when I asked you if you had equipment I wasn't expecting this."

He lifted my favourite, the machine gun with the silencer attached, "Jesus, this is some weapon, I will be using this Boss."

I looked around, the street was quiet but you really didn't know who was watching so I said to Harry, "Right, stick it away, I will let you fire it later on somewhere out in the countryside."

I locked the aluminum shelf down, replacing the rubber mat and closed the boot. We got into the car and took a drive outside the town to a derelict building I used for practise. Harry fired the gun a few times, he was like a child in a sweet shop, he was a real natural, very calm as he pulled the trigger and a very good aim as well so I knew this could work. They wouldn't know what is coming, but we had to make sure we were ready so we drove down to the bar and picked out the best place to park the car where there was only one access point so we could see who or what is coming.

We called into the bar to make sure everything was fine, we had some dinner and at about 8pm I was ready for home. As I left the bar a motorbike just missed me while I crossed the road, it felt like it happened in slow motion. As it passed, the passenger looked around at me and I just caught a glimpse of her: it was Brenda. It was her hair that I noticed, my heart raced as the bike sped off, I ran up the alley to get to the car. It was starting to get dark but I popped the boot, I was in a real panic, I fumbled with my keys and dropped the bloody things. As I bent down to search for them I heard the revs of the motorbike, I reached under the car and started patting the ground and bingo, there they were so I grabbed them and stood up. I looked out onto the main street and saw the bike slowly drive past, I opened the shelf and lifted out the handgun, I pointed it down towards the end of the alleyway and waited. My heart was racing, I was breathing really quickly, I said to myself, "Fir fuck sake Jonny, calm down."

I took a couple of deep breaths and watched and

waited but the bike didn't return, just then Harry came walking around the corner. "Are you ok Boss?" he asked.

"It was them Harry, she was on a motorbike."

"Where are they now?"

"They came back down the street but they didn't see me so I think they left."

"Come on, let's finish this, get me my gun boss, we are going to go after them."

I went into the boot again and lifted the machine gun out, I slammed the boot shut and we got into the car. I started it and drove out of the alleyway and onto the main road where I followed the direction I saw the bike go. Harry was so calm, he kept looking both ways and up each street as we passed them but there was no sign of Brenda and the bike, after about 10 minutes of driving around Benidorm's streets we decided to head back to my house.

As we drove up the motorway we chatted about what had just happened and then just as we were relaxing, the back window of the car was shot out. I swerved across 2 lanes and then another shot and a side window was out, two motor bikes came up both sides of the car and the passengers were firing at us. I slammed the brakes on and we screeched to a halt, this part of the road was dimly lit, as I looked at Harry he was shouting at me, "GO, GO, GO."

I stuck the car in to first gear and as the tyres squealed we shot forward in the direction of the bikes. I went through the gears and we were now nearly caught up, I put my high beam on and could see all four of them. As we got closer Harry put his gun outside the window and as he leant out he started firing at the bikes, they swerved all over the road to try and escape the rain of bullets that Harry was firing. He hit one of them and it spun and tumbled off the road, I watched as the two guys on it rolled and rolled. Harry kept firing at the other bike but he ran out of bullets, he turned to me and said, "Ram them Boss, fir fuck sake hit them with the car."

I put the foot down and as the bike got closer and closer I could see Brenda turn around, she pointed her gun and I could see the flash of it as she fired. I swerved to miss the bullet and accelerated even more to get alongside the bike, just as Brenda went to turn to face me I drove the car right into them and off they came. My car span as well but we eventually came to a halt; we both got out of the car, the road was a mess with debris of the bike everywhere, I raised my gun as I walked towards both of the bodies. I approached the first body, he was moaning and trying to crawl away, I didn't even hesitate, I put two bullets into him and moved on to where Brenda laid. She was taking her helmet off and as she looked up at me she said, "Your family is…"

I knew what was coming, I had heard it all before, I just squeezed the trigger and blew her fucking head off and it was done.

I turned to Harry, "Come on, let's get out of here."

We both ran to the car and sped off, when I got the car up to about 80 I banged the steering wheel, "Yes, we did it Harry."

Harry turned to me, "Boss, I'm hit."

I turned to look at him and saw that he held his shoulder, he then showed me his hand which was covered in blood. "Shit Harry, keep pressure on it, we will get you to hospital."

"No boss, we can't go to the hospital. Take me to yours, I will be ok."

"You need treatment, you need to get to the hospital."

"No hospital boss, we will be arrested, just get me to yours and I will make a phone call."

I put my foot down and as I headed for home Harry lifted his phone out and made a phone call. He gave the person on the other end of the phone my address and told him what to bring.

I got home in about 15 minutes and Harry was losing blood fast, I jumped out of the car and ran around and got him out; I helped him in to the house and he lay down on the settee, I went to the drawer in the kitchen and got a pair of scissors and went back to the living room and cut his top off to reveal the extent of his injuries. He was covered in blood and starting to lose consciousness, I kept talking to him as I went to get clothes to clean the blood away. I was in a real panic trying to get him cleaned up to see where the bullet went in and then I heard a voice from behind me, "Watch out of the way, let's get a look at him."

I stood up and turned to see this wee man with a bald head and round framed glasses, he was carrying a leather bag. As he walked towards he said, "I take it you are Jonny, my name is Edward, can you get me a basin of hot water and clean towels please?"

He was really calm and his tone was reassuring, I went straight into the kitchen and boiled the kettle. I lifted half a dozen clean towels out of the cupboard and when I went back into the living room he had Harry on the floor and was injecting him with something, I set the basin of water and towels beside him. He looked up at me and said, "Thanks very much, have you got any vodka in the house?"

I replied, "This is no time for a drink, for fuck sake, fix Harry."

He smiled as he said, "It's to clean the wound, you can have a drink after."

"Oh right," I said as I went to the unit beside the TV, lifted out the bottle of vodka and handed it to him. He took it and said to me, "Relax Jonny, Harry will be fine, now just take a seat."

I sat on the blood stained sofa and just watched as Edward got on with helping Harry.

He lifted one of the towels and soaked it in the hot water, he didn't even flinch as he rang it out and began to clean Harry up who was moaning a bit. He then rolled Harry onto his side and as he wiped his back he said, "It's a clean shot, it went straight through, just a few stitches required."

He rolled Harry over onto his back and then lifted the bottle of vodka and a towel, as he poured the vodka onto the open wound Harry winced in pain. Edward said, "Now come on big lad, you have had worse than this, just bite your lip and get on with it." As he wiped the bullet hole he lifted his bag and said to me, "Can you set all this stuff out on the table for me Jonny?"

"Yes, no worries."

I lifted his bag and set it on the table and began to unpack it, when I finished I sat back down on the sofa and just watched as Edward lifted a needle and thread and began to stitch the first bullet hole up. He then turned Harry over and stitched the exit wound up, he covered both wounds with a pad and tape, then injected Harry again and said to me, "Can you give me a hand to get this big fella to bed? He needs rest."

Harry was a big lad and we both struggled to get him to my bedroom and into bed. When we went back into the living room Edward packed his stuff up and said his goodbyes, he told me he would call tomorrow afternoon to check on him but told me Harry should be ok. It amazed me that he didn't even ask how Harry got shot.

After Edward left I closed the front door and the realization of what had happened started to sink in. My living room was in a state, there was blood soaked towels lying on the floor and the sofa was covered, it was just a mess and I needed to get it cleaned up.

I started by filling a black bin bag with the towels and other stuff that Edward had used and then made an attempt to clean the sofa, but it was useless, it was ruined and I would have to order a new one.

As I sat on my knees with a scrubbing brush trying to get the blood out of the sofa cushions I wanted to ring Karen, I looked at my watch and it was 11.15pm which would make Belfast time 10.15pm so I lifted my phone and dialled her number. She answered straight away, "Hi love, how's it going?" her voice was lovely, if only she knew what had happened.

"Just having a cup of tea before I go to bed, how's the kids?"

"They are grand, I can't wait to see you."

"I know love, I miss you as well, how's the Christmas shopping going?"

"All done, just putting the time in, what time do you get here on Friday?"

"I will be there by lunch time, I'm on the first flight out."

"Aw that's good love, means we can take the kids to see Santa. There is a really good one in Castle Court."

"I look forward to that, I will give you a ring tomorrow, love you."

"Ok, love you too."

I hung the phone up and went out and put the bin bags in to the boot of my car, which was a bloody mess as well. The windows were shot out and one side of the car was damaged where I hit the motor bike. There was nothing I could have done to fix it so I just went back in to the house and checked on Harry, he was fast asleep so I decided just to go to bed myself.

The next morning I went straight in to see Harry and surprisingly enough he was lying awake and looked fine.

"Alright mate, how are you feeling?"

"I'm ok Boss, just a bit tired and sore, but apart from that I'm bloody starving. Have you anything for breakfast?"

"Fuck me Harry, after what you have went through you're hungry?"

"A man has got to eat Boss."

I just laughed and said, "I will rustle you something up."

As we sat and had breakfast the door rapped, I got up and answered it and it was Edward back to check on Harry.

"You must be ok Harry if you are having breakfast."

"Yes Doc, I'm fine, what's the damage?"

"Just the usual Harry, a grand."

"No worries, I will get it to you later."

"That's fine." He went into his bag and lifted out a bottle of tablets. "Take two of these four times a day for a week Harry and then give me a ring and I will get your stitches out."

"That's super Doc, and thanks for everything."

"It's just business as usual with you Harry," he laughed and then lifted his bag and left.

"Fuck me Harry, what are you involved in?"

"I told you before Boss, I have a history, but that's for another time. Now don't be letting your breakfast go cold, get tucked in."

I was gob smacked but I sat down at my table and had the most unusual breakfast I had ever ate.

CHAPTER 25

Home For Good

After breakfast I had the conversation with Harry that I was going to go home as soon as I could get a flight but that I needed him to get the car fixed and get rid of any evidence that could tie us to the shooting. Again, nothing was a problem to him and it give me peace of mind knowing that I had someone I could trust to clean up any mess I was in.

I paid his doctor's bill and left him some cash to get things fixed up. I then went onto the internet to check for flights and booked one for the next day, I thought it would be a nice surprise for Karen to get back a couple of days early.

We left the car at one of Harry's mate's garage to get repaired, again it was 'ask no questions just cash in hand' and I borrowed a car from them to run about in.

When I dropped him off home I thanked him and told him I would ring him on Friday to check up on things.

I drove down to the bar and met with Peter and Paula to let them know I would be away for a couple of weeks, all they could talk about was the shooting, it was all over the news. It was being linked to the dissident I.R.A and an internal fall out, Peter was all into it, he said to me, "Jonny, I believe it was a high speed chase and that there is three dead with one in hospital fighting for his life."

He grabbed my attention when I heard him say that, *'Fuck,' I thought, 'what if he comes around and names me and Harry?'* "Sounds serious Peter, and right here on our door step, you aren't safe anywhere," I replied worriedly.

"I know Jonny, you're probably right heading home for a while. God knows what will happen next."

"Paula, are you ok to run things while I'm away?"

"Take as long as you need Jonny, everything will be fine."

"When I get back we will set that meeting up with Carlos and get you both in as partners, something to look forward to for next year."

"Yeah, I think I can speak for both Peter and I, we can't wait to put our stamp on the place."

"That should be fun, look, here is a wee something for Christmas for you both for all your hard work." I handed them both an envelope with 500 euro in each.

"Thanks Jonny, have a nice Christmas break and we will give you a ring if we need you."

"No worries, have a nice break yourselves and don't be over doing it with the eggnog."

We all laughed and I left to go and get Karen something for Christmas.

I drove to a local jeweller's, Karen loved her bling so I decided to buy her a lovely necklace and bracelet set. It set me back a bit but she was worth it, he even threw in matching ear rings which surprised me as they were priced at 60 euro. He must have made a bit from the set if he was able to give me the ear rings for free. I got him to put them in a lovely display box and wrap them up with a red bow to finish it off, I was really pleased and I thought Karen would be too.

I drove up home but on the way called into a café just around the corner from our house and had some lunch. As I sat waiting I watched the TV, the news was on and it was reporting on the shooting and the guy talking released the names of the dead. He named the three that I knew I had killed then the guy reporting held his hand to his hear and said, "Breaking news just in, a fourth man who was fighting for his life in hospital has just died. All four assailants were connected to the I.R.A and Police are looking at it as an international incident and will be working closely with the British and Irish government." I had a smile on my face.

The girl then came down with my lunch and said, "Lasagne and chips sir?"

"Yes, that's it, could I get a tin of *Coke* please?"

"Certainly."

I was pleased as punch, no loose ends and heading home the next morning, I put salt and vinegar on my chips and got stuck in.

I headed for home and packed my bag and as I sat

watching a film on TV my work phone rang. "I wondered when you would ring," I said.

"Super result, a job well done, I hear you are taking a break for a while?"

"Yeah, to spend time with the family."

"I want you to take a break for a long while, when I need you I will contact you but go and enjoy life for a while. Destroy the phone and go back to normal life."

"Normal life? I will never have a normal life, this is who I am now and it feels good clearing the scum of the planet so whenever you need me I will be waiting."

"Your normal payment will be processed tomorrow and a bit extra to keep you going, you will receive a monthly income but just remember you work for me and only me."

"I understand, I wouldn't have it any other way."

"Goodbye, I will be in touch."

Drew hung the phone up and I just smiled. I took the phone apart and removed the sim and cut it up and threw it in the bin. I walked outside with the bin bag and put it in the large bins on the other side of the road, job done.

I spent the rest of the day lazing about and then went to bed around 11pm, I was due to go to the airport around 10am in the morning and couldn't wait to get my arse on that seat on the plane.

The next morning I left the key of the house under the plant pot for Harry so he could get the sofa replaced and keep an eye on the place while I was away. I drove up to his mate's garage and left them their car back and got a taxi to the airport arriving there bang on 10am. I got checked in and as I sat in the departure lounge life was great, I couldn't wait to get back to Belfast and see Karen and the kids.

I checked my online banking and my eyes widened as I saw the balance, I looked and looked to see if it was what I was really seeing - my balance read 560,495 euro. I couldn't contain my excitement, I had such a smile on my face and said to myself, *'This is going to be a good Christmas.'* I logged off and put the phone in my pocket and for about an hour I just sat smiling, I'm sure anyone looking at me would think there was something wrong with my head 'cause I would have thought the same, but I didn't care I just sat there grinning.

My flight was called and I was on my way, two and a half hours later and I was landing in Belfast city airport and the site of the big cranes was super to see, I was home.

A short journey up the Hollywood road and I was at Karen's mum and dad's house. As I lifted my bag out of the taxi's boot, Karen came running across the street. "You're home!" she said as she threw her arms around me.

"Jesus, you would think I'd been away for 6 months," I replied as I hugged her. She kissed me and we walked over to the house, her mum and dad had the kids and god love them, they were really excited to see me. "There's my wee angels," I said as I gave them a kiss. "Hi Alan, hi Sandra, how are you both?"

"All good Jonny, kids have been super but Karen

was really worried about you. Is everything ok?" Alan asked.

"Couldn't be better Alan, I hear you have a beer with my name on it."

"I do son, come in and I will pour you one."

No matter when we were home Alan always had a beer in the fridge and I enjoyed the craic.

Karen had a thousand questions but after a while, and a couple of vodkas I may add, she calmed down and we had a nice afternoon with her mum and dad.

We got chippers for dinner and with having a few beers, I was starving. I'd forgotten how good fish and chips tasted back home with bread and real butter, and to top it off: a tub of mushy peas, the food back home was definitely one of the things I missed.

The next day we took the kids into Castle Court to see Santa and what a disaster that was, Erin just squealed when we sat her on his knee, and then there was Josh… I swear if I was Santa I would have filed an assault charge, he absolutely mauled him, his beard ended up round the back of his neck and as for his rosy red cheeks, his whole face was beetroot red. He had the patience of a saint. By the time I trailed Josh off him he was a mess but it was an experience I will never forget.

On the Friday I phoned Harry to make sure everything was ok and to check the bar was getting closed up for the Christmas period. He told me everything was quiet and that I wasn't to worry about the bar, which was what I was wanting to hear.

"Have a nice Christmas and don't be drinking too

much."

"I will Boss, you do the same. I will see you when you get back."

I hung the phone up and told Karen everything was ok back home.

She said to me, "Jonny, we need to talk about home."

"What do you mean love?"

"Since we have been back here I didn't realise how much I have missed home."

"I know love, the weather is crap here, it's bloody Baltic."

"You don't understand, I mean here, I have missed here."

I paused, "Are you saying what I think you're saying?"

"Yes Jonny, I want to come home."

"Suppose it is doable, we could just keep the house in Spain as a holiday home and buy something here. I could travel back and forward to keep things going with the bar, Paula and Peter can run it along with Harry."

Karen held my hand, "You're not disappointed then?"

"No love, as I told you before I would live anywhere with you and if it is here in Belfast then so be it."

"Jonny that's brilliant, I love you."

"I love you too, we will get Christmas out of the

way then go house hunting."

It was going to be a new chapter moving back home to Belfast but I was looking forward to it. By the time Christmas morning came I was more excited than the kids, it was the look on Karen's face when I gave her the set that I had bought that made it for me though, it was priceless. The thought of staying was even more exciting though, and to be honest, I knew I was home.

BY THE SAME AUTHOR ALSO AVAILABLE ON AMAZON:

JONNY THE BOY FROM THE ROAD

PAYBACK JONNY'S REVENGE

Printed in Great Britain
by Amazon